A Nurse With A Niche "Financial Health"

Dedication

First and foremost, all my work is dedicated to the legacy of my family: my children, grandchildren, great-grandchildren, sisters, brothers, nephews, and nieces. My dream is that our lineage will be forever remembered as an example of leadership and a guide to other African American families to building wealth for themselves and others. Most importantly is that the formula for being the example will be based on each member's personal vision and goals.

Secondly, and more specifically, this book is dedicated to all nurses who aspire to fulfill their lifelong dreams, both in and outside the nursing industry. This book is dedicated to the nurse or individual who wants to find, master, and dominate his or her NICHE while working as a nurse, transitioning out of nursing or any other career. Above all else, this book was written for the person who wants it all and to live his or her best life.

TABLE OF CONTENT

A Nurse with A Niche

"Financial Health"

BY: Donna Rosby MBA, RN

I. What is a NICHE and how do you find yours? (Niche is pronounced "neesh")

Niche is derived from the Latin word "*nidus*", which means 'nest'. It then transferred to the French word "*nicher*", which means 'make a nest'. In the early 17th century, it became known as "*niche*", which means 'recess'.

The dictionary definition of niche states it as "*a specific area of marketing which has its own particular requirements, customers, and products.*"

Donna's definition of niche is "*your specialty, your lane, your brand*".

A Niche market is a specialized area or distinct segment of a market.

The steps to finding your niche can include:

1. Evaluate your passion and skills
   a. What are you already good at?
   b. What do people come to you for?
   c. If you had all the money in the world, what would you be doing?
   d. What do people tell you that you are already good at?
   e. What are your learned and innate skills?
   f. What skills have you learned through work?

2. Find out if there is a market for your product or business
   a. Ask friends and family if they would buy your product?
   b. Perform a Google keyword search.
   c. Check if there are already apps for your idea.
   d. Are there any books on your topic?
   e. Remember that just because there may not be a market now, does not mean you cannot create the market. Or, if there already is a market, that doesn't mean you can't join it.

3. See if you can narrow your Niche
   a. Is there a subcategory?
   b. Is it a male vs. female dominating area?
   c. Is it 'job description' based?
   d. Is it race based?

   For example, my niche starts with nurses because I am a nurse, so I can relate to nursing as a category.

4. Check out the competition
   a. Follow others who are doing what you want to do. What are the differences between your idea and your competitor's?

5. Test your niche, let your audience tell you what they want
   a. Use a landing page to allow you to see interest
   b. Use surveys
   c. Give away freebies and get auto responses to your test product.

II. Introduction

My desire for this book is to help you to find, maximize, and/or walk in your niche. Now that you have a better understanding of what a niche is, let's find out how to expand on the idea and begin to generate profits from your dream as a 'Nurse with a Niche'.

My experience has taught me that your niche is probably already a part of your DNA. As with any stage in life, there are learning points, experiences, obstacles, challenges, and opportunities that relate to your story.

As a child, you learned how to brush your teeth. Your parents probably made you brush them after every meal. If they never taught you *how* to brush your teeth -though you may be able to brush your teeth today- your technique could be wrong. This could result in tooth decay. This is an example of how reinforced learning can lead to long term, positive results. And how each phase of the learning process can result in varied outcomes both good and bad, whether the learning is momentarily or constantly.

This application applies to nursing as well. To become a nurse, we all had to study science. Each person's study habits are different. Those differences come from either how you learned to study or how you developed new study habits while in nursing school. In high school, my study habits were very bad. However, I learned new and effective study habits from seasoned "A" students in college. This resulted in my success in college and nursing school. If your style of learning led to success, it probably stayed with you. Your study habits are an example of a learned skill which laid a solid foundation for the success of your future studies.

Now, how can we apply this to business? If you are reading this book, you either have a niche idea that you want to turn into your career, or you want to maximize the niche you are already in. By understanding what you want and can do with your business niche, it will bring you one step closer toward your niche dream.

I will tell you my story as an example of how my life led me to my business niche and ultimately to financial well-being. *"How did you go from nursing to money?"* This is the question I am asked all the time. In retrospect, I didn't go from nursing to money; money was always there for me. My niche helped me find it.

My job was to accept that my niche was what I was supposed to be doing, and to continue to master the gifts that were intrinsic aspects of the success of my niche and my life.

In my story, the points of interest and names are explained in detail. Hopefully, this will help you to better understand the dynamics of your story and how the hidden gems of your future are already embedded in your story. Hopefully, you too will be able to examine your story and better find and understand your niche after reading this book.

My Story

There was a light skinned, tall, thin, fourteen-year-old young lady named Mary, who went by the name "Mayola". Mayola dated a sixteen-year-old young man named Victor, and eventually gave birth to their first born, Donna. Mayola had a sister named Gertie and a close friend named Evelyn. So, when Mayola became pregnant, Evelyn asked to be Donna's Godmother. Donna was born on Evelyn's birthday. Everyone was so excited and knew that Evelyn should be the godmother to Donna.

At the time of Donna's birth, Victor and Mayola were young and extremely poor. They lived with Mayola's mother, Lela, in a 2-bedroom apartment in the Oakland, California projects area, along with 5 other members of the family, for two years. Eventually, Victor could not take Lela's strict living environment and moved Mayola and Donna to a close-by, one-bedroom studio. The small family struggled tremendously, often going without food and having their utilities shut off. Victor worked many small jobs, trying to support his teenage girlfriend and daughter. It was one and a half years later when Mayola became pregnant again and had a son, Victor Jr, when Mayola was sixteen years old and Victor was eighteen years old.

Evelyn's mother "Doll" and stepfather "James" had no children together and were close friends of the family. James graduated high school and went on to a successful career in the military. Later, Doll became a day worker. Evelyn was closer to Mayola's older sister, Gertie, and they both protected the younger Mayola.

Evelyn began babysitting Donna for Mayola on weekends and some weekdays. Let's not forget that Evelyn was a young teenager herself. She didn't realize what being a godmother entailed. This every weekend babysitting began to interfere with Evelyn's weekend fun, so she started bringing Donna to her parents, James and Doll, to babysit. They became close with Donna and decided to ask Victor and Mayola if they could help take care of Donna by providing clothes and money as needed, since they did not have small children of their own and had fairly good jobs. Victor and Mayola were living in their studio apartment and struggled to take care of their two small children. They were incredibly grateful for the help that James and Doll offered.

Though James and Doll provided total financial support for Donna from that day forth, they never asked for custody of Donna. Eventually, Donna would stay with James and Doll during the weekdays and with her mother on the weekends.

Donna's life with her parents was quite different from her life with James and Doll. Donna's life with her parents -Victor and Mayola- was chaotic, unstructured, and undisciplined. She had no schedule, no savings plan, and no allowance. While at James and Doll's house, however, structure was primary, discipline was a must, and studying was required. Some requirements with James and Doll included homework after school first before television, reading at least 2 books per week, and saving 20% of her allowance (which at that time was $20.00 per week). This was quite different from her experiences with her mother.

Donna remembers one time, at age 15, when she went with her mother to the check cashing store. Mayola had cashed her check and stuffed all the cash in her purse. She asked Donna if she had any money. Donna replied, *"no"*. Mayola then dug in her purse, grabbed a wad of money, and stuffed it in Donna's backpack. Donna asked her mother *"how do you know how much you gave me; don't you have bills to pay?"* Mayola stated," *take what I give you, buy you something nice"*. It was at that moment that Donna realized she liked the way James handled money. She never wanted to treat money the way her mother had.

As Donna got older, she began to acclimate to James and Doll's lifestyle. James was retired military, so discipline was his norm. Their habits became hers. James' disciplinary style became her style. Donna was nine years old when she began to emulate James' habits. She studied at the same time every day, watched little TV, and went to bed early. She woke up early with James and read the newspaper during breakfast. Although there were many habits taught to Donna while with James and Doll, the most important skill taught to her was learning about money.

These skills would be needed for college, and college was a must - no negotiation! James began talking to her about money and how important it was to understand that working hard was the way to get money. He showed her his paycheck and explained that his overtime was an example of working hard. He would calculate what his paycheck amount should be before picking it up every

10

other Friday. He explained to her what FICA, social security, and taxes were. He then started showing her how these items were automatically deducted from his received balance. Donna learned quickly how to balance his paycheck, and minus the deductions. She became exceptionally good at calculating his take-home dollar amount to the smallest cent.

While James began teaching her about his money, he started giving her an allowance for doing the household chores. Donna saved her allowance, not wanting to spend her money on anything. This changed quickly, when James told her the purpose of an allowance was to get what she needed and not have to ask him, Doll, or anyone else, for money. *"Just spend wisely"* he would say. Donna's allowance was $20.00 per week.

Donna's savings grew to $2,000.00 by age 14 and in the ninth grade. Donna was a straight "A" student in high school and began preparing for college with the dream of becoming a doctor. James and Doll never allowed Donna to work while in high school. All she was allowed to do was to study and read. They believed that you would work until the age of 65 and that work would consume your entire adulthood. So, save working until you had to, or in my case, after graduation.

The only money Donna handled was her allowance. Although James taught Donna about money, Doll would occasionally tell Donna that she would be a good nurse. She would say, *"it's in your DNA and you care for people so well."* This was a random conversation that held no meaning for Donna at the time.

As time passed, there was so much pressure on Donna about going to college that she didn't think about becoming a nurse. She knew she had to go to college, but she wanted to be a doctor. She applied to three large universities and was accepted to all of them. She didn't know what nurses did, but knew she wanted to be in the medical field. Becoming a nurse would be what Doll wanted for Donna but, Donna wanted to make her own decisions about her future. Why? Because she didn't want to be told what to do anymore.

All her life, everything was dictated to her. This time, she was going to take a stand. She didn't realize until adulthood that this was really a plan, a goal, a seed of destiny planted in her mind. Plans and goals are good, but Donna didn't realize it at that time. Often others may see something in you that you don't see in yourself. I know it's hard but, sometimes we just have to trust and listen.

Later, Donna attended UC Davis as a pre-med student. While at UC Davis, she was desperate to get a job and make her own money. Finally, she got her first job at an off-brand shoe store. Unfortunately, she was fired two weeks later because she did not know how to count change. "*How ironic is that,*" she asked herself. "*how can I be such a good saver but can't count money? I must be an idiot in disguise.*" Donna decided at that moment that she would always learn about money, including how to count it. Donna continued to save her allowance and was frugal in her purchases throughout college. She wanted to save everything she earned. She wanted to make James proud of her.

As Donna's life continued, the next moment of "*financial health*" awareness came when she decided that medical school was not attainable because she couldn't count change, as well as getting her first "F" in economics. "*What a dummy I can't be a doctor, I can't even count,*" she thought. Donna changed her major to Dietetics. Afterall, money and medicine didn't make sense, and Dietetics was still close to people. She graduated with a degree in Dietetics. After working as a Dietitian for three months and getting stuck in the kitchen with the cook, Donna knew she wanted to work with patients at their bedside. Unfortunately, it was too late… or was it?

Soon after leaving her dietetics job, Donna had a child. Sadly, after two months of motherhood, she became a single mom after her baby's father was murdered. She went to work at random jobs,

12

ultimately collecting unemployment. She sat on a bench in front of her 600 square foot apartment with her upstairs neighbor. They sat on that squeaky, splintery bench every day for three months until she realized she only had one last unemployment check coming.

She then applied for a job at a bank in customer service and got it. Not on the banking side; her job was on the phone, answering people's loan questions. Eventually, she became bored, depressed, and drowning in debt. What happened to the saving queen, the little girl who counted every coin? Single motherhood and survival had taken it. It was then that things changed.

The bank decided to relocate to another state and give a retirement package to all its employees. Donna took the package and sat on the same bench with the same upstairs neighbor. The retirement package included a $6,000.00 check and a return to school certificate. She looked at that package for two days while lying on her couch. Though this retirement package was an amazing gift and opportunity, she was so stuck in her depression that she couldn't get off the couch. She was a depressed lump!

She never told James and Doll that she lost her job. They thought she was a business banker. It would break their hearts to know that their precious Donna was not a 'success'. At least that was what Donna thought they would think. Then one day, while walking to the laundry mat with her $3.00 laundry allowance, she found a twenty-dollar bill. She quickly picked it up and looked around for someone to ask for it back. That twenty-dollar bill lifted her from her depression and gave her life. It was as though it was twenty thousand dollars.

She woke up early the next morning, energized and inspired. She realized she wanted to be a nurse after all. She wanted to be an ER nurse. She wanted excitement in her career. That was it…an ER nurse. She cleaned the house and started making calls to city colleges. She was determined to use her 'return to school' certificate to better her life and her child's life.

As she started making calls, she soon realized that the certificate from the old job was for 18 months of higher education and nursing school was 24 months for anyone with a bachelor's degree. *"Now what?"*, Donna thought. So, it was back to the couch of depression she went.

Another 3 days passed. It was Monday morning. She woke with a game-changing idea. She decided to appeal the eighteen-month requirement. She appealed and won. *"Nursing school, here I come"*, she screamed and jumped. Nursing school paid in full for 2 years! The nursing school board decided that if she could graduate from UC Davis with a 3.0 GPA, then she was disciplined enough to finish 24 months of nursing school.

Donna soon realized that ER nursing was not for her. It was not as glamorous as she had imagined. It was hard work, long hours, deaths, and many incredibly sad social situations. So, she began to work toward her career as a cardiac nurse.

Oh, I forgot to mention that her mother died of a massive heart attack at the age of 47, during her last quarter of nursing school. This answered the dilemma of what Donna's nursing specialty would be. She became a cardiac nurse. While working as a nurse, it didn't take long for Donna to realize that she still loved numbers. With the money she made as a nurse, she felt as if the fog had been lifted. Now, she had money to provide for herself and her family. She finally had a career that she, James, and Doll would be happy with.

So, to stay close to money, she taught herself how to manage her 401k retirement account. She studied it and read books on it until she mastered it, attaining a 30% return on her portfolio. The other nurses saw what she was doing, and she decided to help them. As her talent grew, more and more nurses sought her help. She wanted to learn more, so she took a business course. That one course was not enough. She wanted to master it. That was it! She wanted her master's degree in finance. So, she appealed to the university to allow her to enroll, since she already had two degrees.

They approved and she got in. Twenty-four months later, she received her MBA in Finance.

Donna wanted to know more than the 401K. As her financial knowledge grew, she developed an interest in the stock market. Donna wondered why it was so mysterious. Why weren't there many others who looked like her teaching it? So, she decided to teach herself. She bought books, listened to webinars, paid for bad courses, whatever it took to learn. Then, she stepped out and bought her first stock, Starbucks. It did terrible, she lost money, so she sold it. She didn't let that sway her; she began buying a variety of stocks.

She was addicted to the stock market and was making a lot of money investing in it. She told others and they wanted to know what she knew. She was only around nurses, so that was who she began teaching first. As they learned more, she found an article on investment clubs. She decided she wanted her own investment club, so she bought a book on how to start one. Hence, her first investment club evolved, consisting of eight of her fellow nurses. Five clubs later, including the first one, she began teaching others how to start their own club and how to invest.

After that, it was like a ball rolling down a hill. Donna took every opportunity that came her way to grow her skills in money matters. This skill base included becoming a licensed insurance agent, a registered tax preparer, a stock club consultant, and later on, an author. All the above licenses were foundational to other educational opportunities. For example, with the insurance license, you have to learn annuities. With the tax preparer license, you have to know the tax laws. With all of them, you have to understand budgeting. There you have it, "All things money" was her birth right, born from the cards life dealt her.

This is the story of Donna Rosby and her journey from nursing to finance. For Donna, finance was her niche outside of nursing.

Though nursing is a phenomenal self-sacrificing career, for many, it can be a choice, based on a passion for wanting to help others. It can be a lifelong dream or maybe even a choice, based on attaining financial security. After all, it's a known fact that nurses are paid very well. However, regardless of why you chose nursing, you may still desire a career outside of nursing at any point in time. This could be your niche.

Donna's journey is uniquely hers, just as your journey is, and will be, uniquely yours. However, there is a universality that connects all our journeys. We all have our struggles to overcome. We all have our successes to celebrate. We all have our unique niches to find, develop and grow. We all journey down our life's path toward attaining our purpose in life.

What's your story?

As you've read earlier, Donna's story is based on her life. Your story will be based on yours, and all the factors intertwined within. As you start to think about your new-found niche, or an already established well-seasoned niche, where do you go from here? In any case, you start with your 'WHY'. Start by asking yourself some questions. If you want to change your career into something else, why do you want that change? These questions have to be addressed because a desire for change is not enough. Your change has to begin from a drive inside you. Also, it must solve a problem or provide a valuable service for your customer. It has to appeal to their needs. Or, maybe you want to improve what you already have... why? How is your improved product or service going to impact others? Will the improvement warrant the time and money it will take for your market followers to follow you? Do you want to leave nursing all together or expand your niche within nursing? Have you ever thought of doing something totally different from nursing? If you could do something different, what would it be if

16

you knew how, or if it was offered with free training? Where would you start? Answering these questions will help you define your niche.

Conclusion

One thing I know for sure is that your vision for your future has to live within you first; an inner drive, strong enough to propel you forward. Your niche will only be the driver for your vision. If you can't see your vision, you will never be it, or have it. Strive to recognize if your vision is attainable and realistic. No one else can tell you what your vision is and how to make it come to fruition. Warren Buffett defines vision as *"a mental model of a desirable, realistic, future state which presently does not exist."* You have to see it first. You have to believe in yourself before others will believe in you. If the tables were turned and you were to look to someone for a product or service, would you believe in them enough to give them your hard-earned money if they didn't believe in themselves?

You are as worthy of accomplishing greatness as the next person. Not only is your vision relevant to your success, your personal vision of yourself is just as important. You have to see in your mind what your future looks like and be able to recognize a clear picture of what YOU will look like in the future. If you don't know what it looks like, how will you know what it is if you find it?

This vision will guide and give you momentum. You'll need to press on when your journey gets tough, or when things don't look like they will work out. This is why your vision has to be yours. It will be with you all the time, via your dreams, thoughts, and imagination. Only YOU will hear the voice of reason when no one else is around, when the going gets tough, when the bills come in, and when you know your product or service will make the

17

difference in someone else's life. Your success starts with YOU! As you cross each barrier, the momentum moves you forward. Because success creates momentum and a strong vision for your future can keep you from sabotaging your success.

Keys to transitioning to your change

I. Finding your niche
    1. Write down the experiences you remember the most in your life in ten-year increments. For example, age 1-10, 11-20, 21-30, 31-40, etc.
    2. Define 1-2 events in each ten-year increment and write it down separately.
    3. Study those 5-6 defined events and see what they have in common.
    4. Write down what people come to you for all the time.
    5. Write down what you are naturally good at.

II. Walking in your niche
    1. Make your niche different, not better.
    2. Make sure your niche has a specific product or service.
    3. Become an expert in the field you choose.
    4. Study your niche market.
    5. Have multiple customers within your niche.
    6. Define multiple ways to monetize your niche.
    7. Don't make your niche too wide.
    8. Talk about your niche all the time.
    9. Market your niche to your defined market the most and to everyone else the least.
    10. Look for funding in your niche market.
    11. Periodically re-examine your niche.
    12. Be ready to pivot your niche in a changing environment.

13. Know your competition to learn what you don't want to do or to do better.

II. Making your niche a business *(Consult an attorney, accountant, or tax preparer!)*

1. Choose your business structure/entity/platform
   i. Sole Proprietor
   ii. Limited Liability Company (LLC)
   iii. Partnership
   iv. Corporation (S or C Corp)
2. Business Formation
   i. State law governs business formation
      1. Find your Business name
         a. Name search done at the state level
         b. Fictitious name (DBA- doing business as)
         c. File for your unique business name
   ii. Federal law governs how you are taxed for federal (IRS) purposes
3. Business Taxation *(see an accountant or tax attorney)*
   i. Sole Proprietor
      1. Schedule C
      2. Uses Employer Identification Number (EIN) or Social Security Number (SSN)
   ii. Limited Liability Corporation
      1. Schedule C - (1 member LLC)
   iii. Partnerships
      1. Schedule 1065
      2. K-1 for members if multiple members
   iv. Corporation (S & C corps)
      1. Form 1120

4. Your team
   (note: you will not need all these at the same time, hire as needed)

   i. Accountant

ii. Attorney
iii. Patent/trademark attorney
iv. Accountability partner
v. Marketing associate

About The Author

Donna Rosby is a registered nurse, author, speaker, serial entrepreneur, and business owner.

She initially started her career working as a registered Dietician before quickly learning that this field was not what she wanted to do. Donna later started nursing school where she graduated, and currently works as a Heart Failure Coordinator after working more than twenty-four years as a bedside cardiac nurse for two different prominent hospitals.

While working as a nurse, Donna began to study areas in the financial sector like taxes, insurance, budgeting education, money management, and the investment clubs. She even self-studied the stock market and began investing. Donna was encouraged with the results of investing and decided to share her knowledge with her fellow nurses by starting a stock investment club thirteen years ago.

The success of that investment club prompted her to open and manage multiple stock investment clubs: The Golden Handshakes, Sisters Seeking Success, Sisters Securing the Bag, and currently a small real estate funding investment club called 'Funding the Block'. She began educating her members on the stock market and empowering them on how to save, invest, and manage money. Donna continued sharing her knowledge of investment clubs by becoming a consultant to others on starting their own clubs.

While studying the stock market, Donna retuned back to school and completed her MBA in Finance. She then started her own company; Mikash Corporation which focuses on financial literacy for children and adults. She also became a licensed insurance and tax agent. Currently, Donna continues to work part time as a heart failure nurse, has a thriving tax business, a financial consulting business, and an investment club consulting business, and a avid investor. As Donna's businesses continue to progress, she continues to broaden her repertoire by authoring five children's books, including a book series surrounding financial principles for children, 'The Mrs. Dollar Series", a book series on financial literacy, "The Wealthy Nurse Series", and a book for nurses, "The Niche Nurse". She also has a t-shirt and product line.

To Contact Donna Rosby:

Schedule a free 30 min appointment with me @

https://mikash.as.me/?appointmentType=16646031

Website: www.Donnarosby.com

Email: info@DonnaRosby.com

FB: DonnarosbyRN

IG:@Donnarosby

You're Going to Be A Nurse!

Tashunna McElveen, RN

At the age of 9 years old, I lived in a small town called Gretna, Va. It is known for the slogan "Ain't nothing big but it's growing." I lived in a well-kept red and white single wide trailer with my mother and my baby brother Charles. It was our home and we loved it. My mother was a widow at a very early age and I reflect back, often wondering how she provided for us so well. Nevertheless, she was a great single mother who made sure we didn't want for anything.

I remember my mother pulling tobacco once but I don't think that lasted long at all. I guess that type of labor wasn't for her because shortly after, I noticed her with textbooks and different types of educational material. Little did I know but she was preparing for her CNA certification. One particular day as I was watching her go through her books, she turned to me and said "you're going to be a nurse." I can still see her pointing her finger at me saying "I want you to go further, you're going to be a nurse" with a big smile on her face. From that moment on, that was all I knew. Tashunna Haley, the little girl from Gretna, VA was going to be a nurse.

I think my journey started as I entered my junior year in high school. I ordered my class ring with a medical symbol on it. Not quite sure of my path, I decided to take a vocational class to enhance my skill set. Going to Vo-tech was the "in" thing anyway in my hometown area. I was offered a CNA class, but I pleasantly declined it because my mother said "I was going to be a nurse". Therefore, I decided to take cosmetology instead. Go figure.

Hence, styling hair played a very intricate role in the development of my nursing career.

At the age of 17, I was taking classes at my local community college in efforts to start perusing my nursing career. I applied to a Registered Nursing program offered by our local hospital and I was denied entry twice. With sheer disappointment, I did the next best thing I could think of and applied to a Licensed Practical Nursing Program. In my mind, I was thinking I would still be a nurse, right?

While attending my LPN program, I worked evenings on Fridays, and all day on Saturdays styling hair as a source of income. This was perfect due to the rigorous nursing program that I attended. The program that demanded all of my spare time. This was pretty tough for an 18 year old. Nevertheless, I was on my way.

I successfully graduated from my nursing program at the age of 20. What a proud moment this was for me! The magnitude of this accomplishment was out of this world to me. I'm about to be a nurse, I thought to myself! I immediately started my job search as an LPN Applicant until I successfully passed my boards, of course. With luck on my side, I was hired at a local rehabilitation center to start off my career. After working for a few months and gaining some experience, it was now time to go face the music.

I remember traveling to Greensboro, NC with a group of students who graduated with me to take our state board examination. The intensity of sitting behind a computer for so many hours answering question after question was draining. I took the maximum number of questions which was 200 and some odd questions. Once we all completed the examination, we discussed the questions we had while traveling home. I remember feeling sick to my stomach. I recall thinking, I didn't put that answer. Granted we all had different tests, we still had some similar questions. In that moment, I felt as if I failed my NCLEX-PN examination. I was physically sick for the next 72 hours while awaiting my results. I remember two of my friends calling in on the 3rd day to find out they had successfully passed their exams. It was now my turn. The feeling of impending doom was all I could feel. As I dialed in to get my results, I could feel my stomach getting weaker and weaker by the second. My palms were sweating profusely. "Lord, please give me strength", I said. As the automated system announced my results, I said this surely couldn't be. There's no way this happened. I hung up and called back again with a little more aggression and eagerness this time. I wanted to make sure I heard things correctly, and sure enough it was the exact same thing I heard the first time. I failed my state board examination. Disappointment and embarrassment took over my entire being. What would I do now? How would I tell my mom, my family, friends, and peers that I failed? How would they look at me?

I had to swallow my pride and tell my Supervisor I was unsuccessful at passing my boards and because of this, I had to resign as an LPN Applicant. Fortunately, I was able to continue working as a treatment nurse for a couple of weeks. I'm not sure how that was legal, but I did it until I found out I was pregnant. Once I was pregnant, everything about wounds made me sick. It didn't matter if they were red with healthy tissue, or foul and infected, they all made me sick.

So reluctantly, I resigned as a treatment nurse. What would I do now? I'm 20 years old, pregnant, living at home with my mother, and no way to pay my bills. My bills weren't a lot, but they were a lot for me.

I did what I knew best; I resulted back to styling hair again. The money was good enough for a while to maintain my bills, but I lost a lot of clientele once I started working as an LPN Applicant. I had to do something different. I was only able to make ends meets. With no extra money and now being on public assistance, I felt like a failure. I wasn't proud but I needed the public assistance for prenatal care. It's only temporary, I reminded myself.

At five months pregnant, I went to work at a very popular mill in Danville, VA. Many know it as Dan River Mills. I was offered a 3rd shift position working 12am-8am, Monday through Saturday. Something was better than nothing, I thought. At this time, it'd been approximately 5 and a half months since I failed my boards. I didn't want to retry. I was too afraid of failing again. So working at the mill was my plan until I figured out my next move. I worked my scheduled shifts and things went well for the first week or so. But as time passed, something began to shift for me. I knew this wasn't for me. I was working on a line with older ladies that had strong personalities. That didn't bother me because I was a little firecracker myself, but to avoid conflict, I simply did my job and went home. I took my lunch when told and I took my breaks when told. I can remember watching the clock and thinking "this can't be it." I can't do this for the rest of my life.

I started calculating how much money I needed to simply get by because a change had to come!

After 4 paychecks, I quit. No resignation, no good bye, nothing. I was out the door and I didn't look back.

Working there changed everything for me mentally. I knew that experience was my push to revisit my nursing career. With the 4 paychecks, I was able to make 4 car payments and pay my insurance for 4 months. This would carry me until after I had my baby and my Mom would make sure I'm fed, of course.

I began to study for my boards while out of work. Now, I had more inspiration to pass my boards because I had a baby to take care of. I was more motivated than ever. I resubmitted my application and waited on my test date.

7 months pregnant, I'm sitting in the testing center once again. I was very nervous and I guess this caused the baby to move more. I would sit back and rub my stomach in an effort to calm us both down. I remember the testing center employee walking over to me and asking if I was ok. I nodded yes and told her the baby and me were both very nervous. She smiled, patted my shoulder, and

proceeded to move along. Once I completed the minimum amount of questions, I left the testing center puzzled about the last question. When testing, the last question is always important and this questioned had me so baffled. It asked me what are some of the physical characteristics of someone with Marfan disease. I will never forget this question because as new graduate I had never heard of this disease. But before I could travel home, it was urgent that I stop by a bookstore to look up what the physical characteristics of someone with Marfan disease was. I couldn't wait, it was like something pulling at me to find out. So, I found the closest bookstore and went searching for answers. As I sat in the store floor flipping pages to find this disease, I knew my answer was going to determine if I passed or failed my exam.

As I read about the rare disease that affects fewer than 200,000 cases a year, I knew the Lord was with me. I answered the question correctly! My heart was so relieved. The answer being abnormally long fingers and disproportionally long arms and legs. As I continued to sit in the floor of the bookstore, I felt at peace with tears in my eyes. I was almost certain that I passed my boards.

Nevertheless, the 72-hour wait was still treacherous, but when I made that phone call this time, things were very different from before. The automated system announced my success! Of course, I called again in excitement to hear that I was successful. The joy I felt in that moment was indescribable. I was finally a nurse, I thought to myself. I was so excited because now me and my baby were on our way!

My car payments and car insurance were all paid, thanks to the paychecks from the mill, but now my baby needed some baby stuff. I had to get a job before the baby came. So, I asked my mother for her JC Penny card and I purchased the most sophisticated black pants suit I could find. We all know black makes you look smaller!

After submitting a few applications, I went for an interview at a Nursing Home in Yanceyville, NC. The interview went very well and of course, I never mentioned my pregnancy. I was asked to start my orientation within the next few days and I gladly accepted.

While in orientation, I walked past the Director of Nursing who interviewed me. I was in uniform and to tell you the truth, I looked very pregnant in that moment. It was like I grew over night. She looked at me very confused and shocked. She asked "where did that come from?' And I asked her "what are you talking about". She went on to say "where did that stomach come from?" It was then I informed her that I was almost 8 months pregnant. I said "you couldn't tell?" Her lack of response and the confused look on her face led me to believe that she could not tell! Oh well, I'm was happily employed at that point.

I had successfully passed my boards and I was hired as an LPN! I had never been so excited about walking through nursing home hallways. I ended up working as an LPN for about 4 years. After doing some travel nursing at a hospital, I realized I had so many restrictions on what medications I could and could not administer. This constantly kept me in search of a "Registered Nurse" the majority of my day. So, I started entertaining the thought of going back to school. I considered applying to the school that had denied me entry twice, but I quickly decided against their program.

I loved working at the hospital in Roxboro, NC as a travel nurse, and one day some students were on our floor for their clinical rotations. I began talking with the students and inquiring about their program. This could be good, I thought to myself. The next day I remember calling Piedmont Community College and speaking to the Director over the Nursing Program. He was like a breath of fresh air. It was as if he wanted me to attend their school. This was a very different experience from the previous schools I attended or attempted to attend.

He gave me the motivation to move forward with my decision. The entry process was so easy, being that I was already an LPN. I entered the program the very next semester, but before I started I had to consider everything, because it wasn't just me anymore.

Now things were going to be a little different this time around because I now had a family which included 2 children. Granted I was excited about advancing my education. However; I still felt a tremendous amount of guilt. I hated the fact that I would always be at school, studying for school, or trying to make a couple of dollars while not in school. When would I have time for my children?

My kids were 2 and 4 years old when I made my decision to return to school. The thought of me not being available for them as needed truly bothered me. I remember speaking to this older lady about my concerns and she said to me "Tashunna, this is the best time to go to school because your children will not remember. However, if you wait until they're older, things will only be a lot tougher." That seemed to make sense to me after pondering over it for a while. It was only a short term sacrifice and by the time they would start school, I would be almost finished!

I still couldn't totally move forward with my plan just yet. I needed to make sure that my parents would be my support system, as well as their paternal grandparents. Having their support meant everything to me because I knew that my children would be in the best hands ever. I knew I would truly need them. After discussing my plans with them, they all gave me their blessing. That gave me the peace I needed to feel comfortable about my decision.

Ok, now that my first concern was satisfied, I could now address my second concern. MONEY! I knew I would have to resign from my LPN position. I had some money saved, but not nearly enough to cover tuition, bills, and gas for the next year or so. "What would I do now", I thought?

I had to result back to what I knew best; styling hair! Styling hair a couple days a week was good for my school schedule, but it wasn't nearly enough income to cover my expenses. Nevertheless, I had to make a decision because the clock was ticking. I stepped out on faith and registered for my classes. It was now or never. I chose NOW!

My Registered Nursing program was so strenuous, grueling, and demanding! It was the best worst program ever. It was great because of my clinical experiences at UNC Hospitals and the psychiatric hospital in Butner, NC. It was truly an environment for learning! However, living in VA and traveling to those locations made for extremely late nights and super early mornings most semesters. That was not even the half of my issues. The struggles I experienced while attending this program almost broke me mentally. The fact that I had a lot of hungry days, a car that I had to tap on the starter before it would start, and no money for books made things very difficult for me. I couldn't ask my parents for anything else. I had already stretched them to the max. So, I began writing letters to God a few days a week. I needed Him more than I ever knew. He was the only one that could help me through this program and meet all of my needs. My prayer life began to develop during this time and it has shaped me into the person I am today.

With God on my side, I successfully graduated from my program and I successfully passed the NCLEX examination the first attempt. This was the best feeling ever! I was officially a Nurse! I was so excited about getting back to work. I was so broke! I interviewed at a Nursing Home in Greensboro, NC and was offered 25.00/hour. I accepted gladly! I was on my way for sure, I thought!

After accepting my job offer, I was sitting in my truck about to share the news with my parents, when I noticed I had a lot of missed calls. Calls from people that I wouldn't normally hear from. I called my mom and my dad answered. He said "Shunna, you need to come home.' I asked what was going on and my dad reluctantly told me that my brother Charles had been found dead. My brother had been off his military base for a few days, but I never thought in a million years that he would be found lifeless.

In a moment of confusion and fog, I asked him again what he said and he repeated to me that my brother was gone. The loss of my brother Charles was devastating to me. He was my baby brother! We had big dreams, dreams of starting a business together. Dreams of conquering the world together. How would we do that now that he was gone?

The loss of my brother broke me in so many ways. I couldn't even smile without feeling guilty. How can I smile or even have a moment of happiness when my brother has no life? With that being said, the thought of opening a business left me totally. I had no desire to become a business owner without my brother.

That would soon change. God has a way of making us revisit things when the time is right and healing has taken place. After working in Long-term care for a while, I decided to do some home care due to the flexibility. I worked for 2 agencies in Greensboro, NC. The companies were black-owned by women with no medical background. So I began thinking, if they could do it, surely I can do it too. I began researching the rules and regulations for North Carolina and Virginia.

I decided to open a company in Virginia. I invited one of my closest friends to join me in a partnership and she agreed. We decided on a name and did all the preliminary work. While working 40 hours a week, we still did the ground work for our business. It was tougher than we both thought. We struggled with the entire process. Working full time jobs made it very difficult to run the business. However, that source of income was very important. It went towards paying our staff due to delays and errors in our billing submissions. I didn't have the time to truly dedicate to submitting claims, and it was affecting us badly. Nevertheless, I wasn't willing to give up my job. Granted, I was already behind on my car payments and I was also in the process of doing a loan modification due to late payments to save my home. All of my money was going into the business and it was about to be the cause of me losing everything.

31

I began to think this was bad idea. One day upon arrival to my full time job, I was late due to my business. The owner's daughter let me know my services were no longer needed. She terminated me! I remember becoming angry and calling my business partner. I realized that everything happens for a reason. We came up with a plan. My goal was to figure out the billing process for the business while she continued working. My business partner agreed to give me enough money to get through, until I could figure out the billing. Now that I had the time to dedicate, I had to act fast. Within 2 weeks, I was finally able to get the billing correct! When we received our first check for 8,900.00, you would have thought it was for a million dollars. I was excited about our first check, but I was even more excited about the door I had unlocked to our financial freedom. We were on our way now for sure!

We began building our client base, securing private contracts, and hiring like never before. The business was thriving and we were able to finally pay ourselves a decent salary. We were proud of our accomplishments and all was going well for about 2 years. Then things changed. Things changed for us significantly and when it hit us, it hit like a ton of bricks.

We owed the IRS money and they wanted it! We had no idea of the debt we had incurred with the Internal Revenue Service. We had a mandatory meeting with the IRS officer and of course we had lots of questions. We were very lost in that moment. However, the officer didn't have a problem enlightening us. We were behind in our employer tax payments. We would receive the coupons to pay the taxes but we didn't have the money, so we simply placed them to the side. While the coupons were laying to the side, penalties and interest were accruing.

After a 2 year run, we had to make a decision. It was a very hard and grueling decision. We agreed to dissolve our partnership and make arrangements to settle our debts with the IRS. It was a very disappointing time for us. This situation truly tested our friendship, but our friendship was bigger than any business and we survived the test.

As time progressed, I realized I wasn't done as a business owner yet. Nursing is my passion but being an entrepreneur was my dream. Why not put the best of my two worlds back together again? I developed a plan to start a home healthcare agency in my hometown. I had learned a lot from my previous mistakes as a business owner: never to play around with the IRS of course, hiring a creditable CPA, and choosing to contract with a payroll company.

In my planning process, I thought about the death of my brother and our plan to start a business together. What better way to memorialize my brother than by incorporating his name into the business? We would still have our dream together as business owners. I decided on a name and a logo that represented how I felt about my baby brother.

Prince Charles Home Healthcare Agency was birthed! The name felt good. The name was more than just a name to me. It had meaning and purpose. My brother's compassion for the elderly, disabled, and children would continue to live through Prince Charles Home Healthcare.

Prince Charles Home Healthcare Agency has now been serving the community of Danville, VA and surrounding areas for 10 years. Who would have thought a little girl raised out of Gretna, VA who lost her biological father at the tender age of 3 years old would manage a company with 90+ employees? Who would have thought a single mother of 2, who didn't have money for food or books while in school would be the owner of a company with an annual payroll of 1-1.5M? I would have never thought it would be me.

Being a business owner has it rewards, but it comes with a lot of responsibilities and challenges. If you desire to become an entrepreneur whether it's nursing related or not, I would recommend that you do your due diligence in researching your business venture. I didn't have any startup money for my first business and this made my journey very difficult. So, it would be wise to have some working capital in place to prevent you from possibly losing your personal assets like I almost did. You must remember that I was a nurse first with no background in finance, accounting, or business management. Therefore; I had to learn or hire people to assist me in those areas. Remember: if you can dream it, you can do it!

In closing, At the age of 9, my mother saw something special in me. It was her speaking it into existence that made me who I am today -A nurse plus so much more!

About The Author

Tashunna McElveen is the Owner of Prince Charles Home Healthcare Agency, LLC which was founded in 2010. Prince Charles employs over a hundred individuals throughout Southside Virginia. The agency currently houses 3 licensed offices for home care and an accreditation through CHAP for Skilled Nursing Services and Laboratory Services. Tashunna began her nursing career as an LPN in 1998, and in 2003 she completed her studies as a Registered Nurse. Tashunna participates on the board for VAPCP as a Regional Director and is also a member of VAHC. These associations help educate business owners on new regulations and laws for hospice, home care, and home healthcare. Initially, Tashunna was interested in starting a company in North Carolina. However, she thought to herself that by opening Prince

Charles in her own community, she would aid in promoting economic development, create employment opportunities and assist individuals with a medical need. With that being said, Tashunna made the decision to start Prince Charles in her hometown. Tashunna is very proud of Prince Charles' community involvement; from school supply giveaways to feeding, clothing, and providing toys to families during the holiday season. The goal of Prince Charles is to continue to grow, educate, mentor, and develop employment opportunities that will continue to revitalize our community.

To Contact Tashunna McElveen:

Email: Tbauldwin30@gmail.com

Website: www.princecharleshomecare.com

LinkedIn: Tashunna McElveen- LinkedIn

From Business Plans to Legacy Planning

Tamara A. Neely, APRN, PMHNP-BC, FNP-C

Legacy Planning

Legacy planning should be in the back of your mind after you start your business. Legacy planning is a blueprint for how you will leave your assets to your loved ones. How you lived your life will be the legacy that you are remembered for. Legacy planning is important for small businesses. It is best to start early, so that you can determine what will happen to your business and assets. This will ensure that your plans are in order after your death.

It will be important for you to have a will completed. Finding the right financial advisor can be done by searching the internet and asking other business owners whom you know. Legacy planning will help you transfer your wealth by paying the least amount of taxes. When you leave a legacy, your family can build their financial securities and future. This will allow your children and family members to live a better life.

Wealth can be identified in the form of stocks, 401K, real estate, a business, intellectual property and money left behind to make more money and assets. The main way to acquire wealth, regardless of how much money you make, is to live below your means by using a budget. A budget will tell you how much money you have left to invest and pay off debt.

Teaching your family and friends about financial literacy is the key to leaving your legacy behind. My goal is to provide a legacy for my family and family members who I may never meet. We owe it to our future generations because our previous generations sacrificed and worked hard for us to enjoy the freedom of leaving a legacy of knowledge, wealth and sound financial habits. I will leave you with a quote from President Jimmy Carter, "Our greatest legacy is not our accomplishments in life, it's what we can do to help the next generation."

10 Keys to Start a Successful Business to Leave a Legacy

When you start a business, make sure you start on the right path. I started out small with one service and grew it over the years to have a successful business. Make sure you do not sacrifice your integrity for money. I equate having a successful business to having an honorary MBA. You must put in a lot of work to get established. A successful business is not a get-rich-quick scheme. Below are 10 keys that will assist you on the path to a successful business and leaving a legacy.

1. **HIRE YOUR DREAM TEAM.** Hire the right people to work with your team. Make sure you hire people who will run with your vision and have passion for your business. If you hire people who don't align with your vision, this can set your business back years and you may never see success. I have had to fire people who brought too much negativity to the workplace. Remember you can have control of who you choose to hire at your company. Don't be miserable along the journey. Your staff will spend more time with you than some of your family members; therefore, they should be pleasant to work alongside with. If you know you lack a certain skill set, you should make sure to hire someone who excels in what you lack.

2. **FIND A MENTOR.** I was blessed to have a mentor in my house growing up as a child. My father, Charles Alford, Sr. is a successful barber in my home town. He opened the first Black barber shop in Benson, North Carolina when I was in fourth grade. I saw him put in challenging work while working a full-time job. It allowed him to be with family and serve his community. Your mentor needs to have traits of integrity, honesty and a desire to help others. For example, if you are looking to start a family care

home, try to find people in your community who are successful, and have operated a business for at least five years as a family care home. Don't get discouraged if someone does not want to be your mentor or share knowledge with you. Keep trying and pray. Ask God to send you a mentor. If you can't find a mentor, find a peer or hire a coach. Sometimes you will have to invest money in reaching your goals. You can surround yourself with people who are trying to start their own business by attending local SCORE organizations. SCORE organizations have the largest network of volunteer business mentors who will work with you at no cost. They offer online and in-person workshops.

3. **WORK HARD, PLAY HARDER.** In order to have a successful business, you need to work HARD. Some people will have to work a full-time job while starting their business or work part-time. The beauty of attaining success is to enjoy the journey. Take time out to enjoy family, friends and doing a little bit of traveling. It can be as small as having a pampering day where you go to the movies or go out for dinner. Make a habit to work out and eat healthy. Give your mind a break by enjoying an hour massage or a facial. These are very affordable at beauty schools, Groupon or Living Social. Some may want to go to the park and see God's nature. If your funds are limited, walking in the park is one of those things that you can enjoy for free.

4. **NEVER GIVE UP WHEN TIMES ARE HARD.** Put God First and he will carry all of your burdens. It is easy to give up on your dreams because it usually requires a lot of work. Sometimes when you want to give up, go volunteer your time with an organization that aligns with the mission and values of your business. If you fall ten times, it is how you get up on the 11th try that counts. Never give up until your last breath. You don't want to look back on your life wondering what if! Remember to try until you succeed. Never give up!

5. **UNDERSTAND YOUR BUSINESS PLAN.** What is a business plan? A business plan should tell us about your company and projections of growth. You can research sample business plans

to fit your business. I took a lot of free classes offered on how to write a business plan, and I was chosen by Small Business Administration as 1 of the 19 inaugural students in Emerging Leaders (Charlotte Chapter). Also, take free classes at the community colleges or throughout the community. Seek education on the topic of your interest. Always be willing to learn more for your business.

6. **KEEP IT SIMPLE**. Since we have the internet to research what type of business you would want to start, it can get intimidating when you see the success of others. When you start your business, try to keep it simple by perfecting one type of service. I started out doing non-medical home care first, later added case management, and then housing. It would have been too much starting out as a new business and hiring staff in this process. As my biology professor would say, K.I.S.S.=Keep it Simply Simple. Even when keeping your business simple, make sure you are strategic with execution.

7. **NO EXCUSES**. When trying to start your business, you may at times come up with a hundred reasons or excuses why now is not the time to start a business. It may be lack of money, education, time or just self-doubt. It all starts in the mind that you can do it. If you never try, you definitely won't succeed in starting a business. All it takes is faith like a mustard seed. You must step out on faith and put into action the plans to birth your new business. Fear is the biggest reason most people never start a business. Don't use fear as an excuse.

8. **LOVE WHAT YOU DO**. When you love what you do, you are really not working! Try to find a business you can work at all night for free, or work without complaining. Don't start a business that you do not have any interest in keeping long term. Have you ever seen professional athletes leave the game because the desire/love was missing? They left millions of dollars on the table because they would rather be happy and play a sport than be miserable. Always remember to follow your heart!

9. **HAVE THE RIGHT PERSPECTIVE.** Starting your business is like birthing a baby. You need to have a positive experience by having positive people around you. There may be some people saying you should not start a business. You need to know that having this business is an extension of you. You must have the right perspective and not allow negativity from others to abort your dreams or goals of having a successful business. Be confident in all of your goals and when you go out in public to represent your business.

10. **USE S.M.A.R.T. GOALS.** If you are a nurse, then you know all about S.M.A.R.T. goals. They should be specific, measurable, achievable, realistic, and time specific. Use this when starting your business. The S.M.A.R.T. goal can be as simple as coming up with your company name as an LLC with a checking account within 30 days. It should be something that you understand is your goal, and not someone else's goal for you. Remember that you are not trying to keep up with other people. If a goal cannot be measured, it will be hard to track.

Business Beginnings

Growing up in a small rural town outside of Raleigh, North Carolina, I knew I wanted a career where I could help others. After graduation from high school, I attended Johnson C. Smith University (JCSU), an HBCU in Charlotte, North Carolina, on a full scholarship. I majored in biology because of my first mentor, Mr. Hubert Avery. I desired more than "country living and a place where everyone knew you."

After graduating in 1994 with honors from college, I decided I would attend NC A&T State University to get my Masters in Biology. I knew during the first week of class that this was not the path for me. Later that year, I decided to become a medical technologist. I worked five years for one of the largest healthcare systems in Charlotte. After working there, I wanted more hands-on care with patients.

41

I decided to apply to nursing school in 2001 and graduated in May 2003. After working as a nurse in a hospital for three years and working just one day with a home care agency in nearby Gastonia, I decided to start my own business. I worked one day for a non-medical home care agency doing home care assessments. Once the owner told me how successful her business was, a light bulb went off. I would not have to pay someone to be my nursing director; I would be able to save that money, starting out by not hiring a nurse. Eventually, I could pay a nurse to work part-time as the business grew.

I diligently researched and opened my homecare business in five months. I have been in business since 2006. The services we provide are non-medical home care, HIV Case Management, VA Contract housing, and leasing some of our rental properties. We have a very specialized niche where we have been working with the government to help solve some issues that clients have, as well as assessing the medical healthcare system. Our services provide cost effective solutions which saves the government money. Since 2006, we continue to make a difference in our clients' lives.

We provide non-medical home care where Certified Nursing Aides (CNA) or Personal Care Aides (PCA) go into clients' homes to assist with activities of daily living (ADL) and housekeeping tasks. This program is called Personal Care Services (PCS) in North Carolina. The client gets up to 80 hours per month. Additional hours can be obtained if clients have Dementia, Alzheimer's or other memory loss conditions. Community Alternative Program (CAP) provides services for clients in their homes. Assistance with ADL's and housekeeping tasks are done by the CNA staff. HIV case management allows the case manager the opportunity to work with the client one-on-one to assist with ambulatory appointments, medications, and medication adherence. Currently, we have two residential group homes which house male veterans in a transitional type of living. We have been working with Veterans Affairs (VA) since 2012. HC4C also has rental properties which are leased to other companies for passive income. One of our company's future plans for business is to expand our clinic outside of NC to MD and FL. I had an in-home daycare licensed by North Carolina in 2001; however, I closed it when I started nursing school. I have always had the desire to help others learn at any age.

Finding my Purpose

You must find your purpose in life to really exist and use your God-given talents. What is your purpose in life? Have you ever asked why? Why were you born into your family? Why were you born Black, White, Hispanic? Why did you get into an abusive relationship? Why did you have sex with someone you trusted and get an STD/HIV? Why did you get pregnant as a teenager without a husband? What would your life look like without any substance abuse? Why did your business fail? Why did a loved one die? Why did you get divorced? These are some of life's questions that can be the catalyst to starting your own business, or finding your purpose. It has been stated that "if you can find out what your passion is, it could be the linkage to your purpose."

I had a desire at a younger age, to help others. While in college at JCSU, I wanted to be a physician's assistant but this never happened. I was not accepted to Duke University in 1994. I did not have the required hands-on experience in healthcare to get accepted. It was a competitive process. After applying twice to Duke University, I didn't have the desire to be a physician's assistant any more. But God had other plans for me! Twenty-two years later, I attended Duke University as a nurse practitioner to pursue a post-master's certificate as an HIV specialist! When you serve a mighty God, sometimes He gives you things you never desired.

What is success? Success is not about how much money you make, but about how you can change the trajectory of someone else's life. I have been blessed along the way, but only through God's grace. Never measure your success against someone else's.

43

This can lead to jealousy and envy. I found my passion, my "why" and what makes me wake up daily feeling successful.

It can become easy to compare. Comparison will do two things: First, it will make you feel "less than" or inferior; or it will make you feel like you are "better than" or superior. Success does not boast but is humble at all times. You can lose everything that took years to build in a blink of an eye. We have all seen celebrities living high, then lose material items and show signs of mental instability.

My purpose allowed me to care for my brother in August 2016. It brought me peace knowing I was able to spend the last month with my brother when he was placed in Hospice Care for terminal cancer. I was able to be his nurse and show compassion and care with excellence along with my sisters, family and church family. This was my passion in action. I was able to work as an unofficial Hospice Nurse; something I never thought I could do. What God allowed was for me to see my purpose at work. You see, your passion or purpose will allow you to transcend/transform and work in other areas that you did not realize you had the potential to achieve.

Why did I Want to be a Nurse Entrepreneur?

I wanted to be a nurse entrepreneur to help and serve the less fortunate and assist in navigating the health care system. I am blessed to learn quickly and help others. I have helped heal and house hundreds of people by doing business for the past 14 years. Most of my work has been with the government. This is where I was able to work with clients from various backgrounds. People often ask me why I want to work with those who have HIV, or homeless veterans with mental challenges and substance abuse. The answer is that I love what I do and I would not change anything on my path as a nurse entrepreneur. Along the way, I mastered how to do business with the government. I have worked with (Medicaid, HRSA, VA) to serve the clientele who needed me the most.

My Dedication

I have been blessed to be a blessing to others. I have dedicated my career to assisting others with our services or helping other entrepreneurs start their business. My dedication to the field of Nursing has become my ministry. Where else could I make such a profound difference in the lives of people I may not have ever met, unless I started my own business? I was able to do it on my own terms and with my own rules. I am dedicated to the field of healthcare.

How to Do Business with the Government in 90 Days

I started my business, and after getting my home care license as a non-medical home care business, I was able to do work with the government (Medicaid). It took about six weeks to get my provider number for Personal Care Services (PCS) and Community Alternative Program for disabled adults and children (CAP/DA, CAP/C). Working with the government has allowed me to live my life on my own terms. If you want to do business with the government, you must run a legitimate, and legal business. Below are 10 steps to start doing business with the government for a contract.

10 Steps to Start Doing Business with the Government to Leave a Legacy

1. Choose a business name and choose which type of business structure will benefit you. This is where you can consult an attorney. You can choose from a sole proprietor, limited liability corporation (LLC), S-Corporation or C-corporation. Corporations protect your personal assets and give your business a nine-digit tax-ID number. You can go online at https://www.irs-ein-tax-id.com to get your Employer Identification Number (EIN). You can get this number in an email, usually within an hour on the same day if done during business hours. As a sole proprietor, all profits and losses are reported on your individual tax return, and the entity is not taxed. Also, you will have unlimited liability for your business debt as the only owner. If you decide to do an LLC,

you can have one or more owners and you must file and register with your state. In North Carolina, I must file every year and pay $202 electronically. LLCs are liable for investments and protect your personal belongings. A C-corporation requires you to have a board of directors/officers, annual meetings and annual reporting requirements with an unlimited number of shareholders. These are usually large corporations such as Microsoft, Wal-Mart, and Ford. There is double taxation, and dividends are taxed at the individual level if given to the shareholder. Lastly, an S-corporation is required to have a board of directors/officers, annual meetings and annual reporting with an unlimited number of shareholders. S-corps differ from C-corps because the entity is not taxed, and the profit and losses are passed to the shareholders and reported on the individual tax return (Schedule K). Again, talk to an attorney to see which setup for your business is best.

2. Open a bank account. Shop around for a free business account. Make sure you get a folder with a copy of your EIN, Articles of Incorporation, Business license or trade name information. You will need some of this information when opening a bank account. I have free accounts at Wells Fargo Bank and Fifth Third Bank. Do your research.

3. Register your business with Duns and Bradstreet. Duns and Bradstreet gives you a data universal number (D-U-N-S) which is a nine-digit identifier, so other lenders and potential businesses will learn about your business credit or financial stability. You can call 1-866-794-1577 for technical assistance. While free for businesses required to register with the US Federal government for grants and contracts, they will try to sell other products to you. Also, you can complete online at https://iupdate.dnb.com/iUpdate/companylookup.htm

4. Locate your North American Industry Classification System (NAICES) Code. This is a 6-digit code that classifies your industry. Some of the codes that I have used to work with the VA are:

NAICS Code: 623220 -- Residential Mental Health and Substance Abuse Facilities 623990 -- Other Residential Care Facilities

5. Register your business at www.sam.gov. This is something that you can do for free. Make sure you go to the correct website to avoid sites that charge you. Don't use www.sam.com unless you want to pay. You will need to update your business every year at www.sam.gov. If this is not active, you will not be allowed to do any contracts or receive money from the government.

6. Get the necessary insurance to do government contracts. Shop around for the best insurance for your needs. You may work with an insurance broker to find multiple companies to compare several insurance plans at a time. You will be required to obtain insurance at the time of the contract. The solicitation will tell you the required amount of insurance to do the contract.

7. Register your business as a HUBZone disadvantaged business (HUBZone) if your business meets the requirement. If you are a minority female business owner with majority ownership, get your Minority Women Small Business Entity (MWSBE) or Women Owned Small Business (WOSB). There are set-asides for small businesses and the government has a goal of awarding 3%-5% of all dollars for prime government contracts. I have my business as a HUBZone and WOSB.

8. Research for contracts. Go to www.beta.sam.gov. This site you will need to play around with, so you can become familiar with how to search for contracts. You can search by states, NAICS codes, or agencies. You can do an advanced search form to get specific information on a contract in which you are interested.

9. Attend workshops. Sometimes you can find out if local government entities are having workshops to review upcoming requests for proposals or contracts, before the bids are due to be turned in.

10. Apply for a contract if you meet the qualifications. Some may require you to have prior experience. I started doing the VA contracts with limited experience. We have now been doing the VA contracts for the longest in the Charlotte region.

A prayer for your business success

May God bless us daily with our business to help everyone we meet along our journey. Give each one of us the spirit of courage and faith with perseverance as we make new contact with the right customers. Please do not let fear exist, but rather a spirit of faith. May our focus always bring joy to you Father God. Bless us with the right staff so we can make an impact on all of those who we will serve.

Thank you, Father God!

Amen

Each of you should use whatever gift you have received to serve others, as faithful stewards of God's grace in its various forms. Peter 4:10

About The Author

Tamara Alford Neely is the wife of Meredith Neely for 22 years and is the mother of Marc and Makayla. She is a Christian who puts God first in her life. She was raised in rural Benson, North Carolina and currently lives in Charlotte, NC. She serves as the Medical Director for her clinic and non-medical home care business. She has been a Nurse Practitioner since 2014. She is an HIV Specialist receiving her training from Duke University. She has been in business since 2006 providing non-medical home care services, HIV case management and housing to male veterans with mental health/substance abuse issues.

Tamara has been a Nurse since 2003. She received her training from Carolinas College of Health Sciences, Winston Salem State University, UNC at Charlotte, and Duke University. In May of 2019, she graduated from Anderson University and now works as a Psychiatric Mental Health Nurse Practitioner (PMHNP). Before nursing, Tamara went to JCSU to obtain a BS in Biology and worked as a Medical Technologist in the hospital for five years.

Her training was done at Carolinas College of Health Science for Medical Technology to work as a Generalist Medical Lab Technologist.

Tamara started her 501 (c)3, The RISE Project of the Carolinas, in July 2008 to start doing government contracts with HRSA. Her first government contract was with Mecklenburg County Health Department, doing emergency financial assistance and case management while working with the community of minorities who have HIV. She has received many grants/contracts since 2008 and written grants for other companies.

She has opened two family care homes and two multi-family housing facilities with services in Charlotte, NC. She has a real estate company -Neely Realty & Investments, which provides rental property and commercial properties in the Charlotte area. She enjoys teaching others about first time home ownership. She believes in giving back and helping others.

She serves as a mentor and coach for others in the healthcare business. Her company, HC4C, has given out three scholarships for the past two years to assist freshmen going to college. She is a consultant for those wanting to start a business in the healthcare area and doing business with the government.

To contact Tamara Alford Neely:

Email: tamara@hc4cclinic.com

Facebook: The NursePRAYneur Business Community

LinkedIn: Tamara A Neely

Websites:

www.wingovernmentcontracts.today
www.wingovernmentcontracts.info

www.hc4cclinic.com

www.homecareforthecarolinas.com

Called to Be a Nurse

Dr. Christy Nneka Olloh, DNP, MSN, APRN, PMHNP-BC

Introduction

What is the definition of a **calling**? According to the Webster Dictionary, the noun calling is "a strong inner impulse toward a particular course of action especially when accompanied by conviction of divine influence." Calling to me is a specific path or journey ordained by the heavenly father to everyone on earth. When someone finds their calling, there is an unexplained passion, peace, or joy within their soul. While working within your calling, it may not feel like work. Some people may never find their calling, some may know their calling from childhood, and others may not discover their calling until adulthood. As you read about my journey, please know that you are very capable of achieving your dreams and goals. All you must do is believe in almighty God, find your calling, believe in yourself, envision yourself at the finish line, work hard, rest, and remain determined. If you do not give up, you will reach the finish line.

My Journey

I was born into a family of healthcare providers, especially Nurses. My mom, dad, cousins, brother, uncle, and aunts are nurses. As a little girl, I told myself I would be a nurse one day. As I grew older, I realized my parents worked a lot and worked shifts such as evenings, weekends, nights, and holidays. My siblings and I were home alone most times during those hours. After High School, due to seeing my parents work odd nursing hours and holidays, I changed my mind and enrolled in an Accounting Degree program at a Community College in Rockland County, New York. My goal changed to someday working in Wall Street when I complete the Accounting Degree. Unfortunately, it did not work out. I dropped out after two semesters and wasted my parent's hard-earned money.

I started praying and thinking about what I was going to do next. My parents sat me down and said, "why don't you try Nursing? You told us as a little girl that you would be a Nurse one day." I responded with, "No! I don't want to be like you guys." Later, I decided to enroll in a Nursing Assistant course. During the first few days of the program, the instructor came to me and said, "have you ever thought about being a Nurse? You will be great at it." In my mind, I was thinking, oh no, not again. I left the course during lunch and never returned. Eventually, I enrolled in an Associate Degree in Nursing program in North Carolina, and the rest is history.

I have been in the Nursing career path for more than fourteen years. Along the way, I found my **calling** to serve the mental health population. Within the past five years, I have been practicing as a Family Psychiatric-Mental Health Nurse Practitioner and teach other Nurse Practitioners how to open and run a successful private practice. To God be the glory, I own and operate Maricopa Christian Psychiatry Group DBA Maricopa Christian Psychiatry in Chandler, Arizona. I am also the owner of GE Psychiatry and Consulting Services, LLC. This long journey has been a lot of hard work, yet humbling. I am incredibly grateful for the opportunity.

Connecting Nursing to Business

My years of experience as a nurse has helped shaped my businesses in several ways. I was the nurse that stayed in my patient's room a little longer to comfort them and make them smile during their hospital stays. I loved talking to my patients and their families but completed my required care and documentation before the shift ended. Every day before I left work, I made sure I touched someone's life. Today, in my private practice, my patients suffering from mental illness enjoy the luxury "quality time," meaning I give each of my patients the amount of time they need to express themselves without feeling rushed, unheard, and judged.

Nursing has helped shape my consulting business by helping me learn how to be very patient and accommodating. I spend the quality time needed by my clients to help them achieve their goals. I encourage my clients to believe in themselves, no matter how anxiety-provoking this journey may be. Watching my clients grow and improve at each phase of their business, and seeing how happy they are providing compassionate care to their patients brings me joy. I enjoy and look forward to every part of it.

Becoming a Nurse Entrepreneur

In 2009, when I had my first child Gabrielle, I was working as a Registered Nurse. During that time, I was doing eight to twelve-hour shifts at a local hospital in Dallas, Texas. It was difficult to leave our daughter in Daycare for long hours while my husband and I worked. Receiving random calls to pick up my daughter because of one sickness or the other from Daycare staff became tiring. That year, I made up my mind to advance my education. I reenrolled myself in school and began my Bachelor's Degree in Nursing the following year. I continued to further my education by going to graduate school and later found my passion for mental health.

After graduate school, while working as a Nurse Practitioner, I noticed the rush by the mental health organizations I worked for to see many patients. There was a constant push to see so many patients in a day within a short time. This push left some of my patients feeling rushed, unheard, and just another number. I started feeling burned out. I became a complainer, and my passion for mental health started quenching. After praying and talking to my husband, I decided to stop complaining and change the way mental health services are provided. The change had to start with me.

In 2017, my husband and I took a leap of faith to move over a thousand miles away from family to walk away from working for others. I became a Nurse Entrepreneur and broke away from the cycle of a complainer. Now I work with my patients and provide the extra time they need. Adequate time, prayers, along with medication and therapy, helps my patients with healing, recovering, and stabilization. Furthermore, I became a Nurse Entrepreneur to decrease the likelihood of my children going through similar childhood experiences from lack of parental supervision due to odd or long work schedules. I now have the freedom to spend time with my family the way I choose. My family means a lot to me. My children are one of my biggest priorities. Lastly, I am now helping others achieve their dreams and goals.

The Do's and Don'ts Before Opening a Nursing Business

If you are a Nurse or in any other career and want to open your own business, my **Do's** and **Don'ts** recommendations are:

Do's

1. Stop **complaining.**
2. Pray to God for **direction.**
3. Find your **calling** or identify what your passion is.
4. **Learn** yourself. Which means understand your likes and dislikes.
5. Find your "**main passion**" in nursing or your career. Main passion means the part of nursing you enjoy.
   Examples include working with people struggling with drug or alcohol abuse problems; Assisted Living; Home Healthcare, Transitional Housing for people coming out of prison or at-risk youths; people living with HIV, Real Estate for travel nurses, etc.
6. Ask for **help**.
7. Turn your **main passion into a business.**
8. Lastly, be **the change agent** in your chosen business. A change agent is an individual who intentionally makes positive changes in a setting or organization.

Don'ts

1. Do not **give up**, no matter what.
2. Do not be **afraid** to take a leap of faith.
3. Do not **compare** your journey with others.

About The Author

Dr. Christy Nneka Olloh is happily married to a very loving and supportive husband, Emmanuel Olloh, for 12 years. Together they have four beautiful children. She enjoys spending lots of time with family, learning new things, cooking, and traveling. Dr. Olloh has been in the nursing profession for over 14 years. She practices currently in her private practice Maricopa Christian Psychiatry in Chandler, Arizona, as a Family Psychiatric Mental Health Nurse Practitioner. Dr. Olloh is licensed to assess and treat patients across the life span for Psychiatric Disorders, not limited to Anxiety, Depression, Attention Difficulty, Psychosis, and Bipolar disorders. Dr. Olloh also owns and operates GE Psychiatry and Consulting Services, LLC, to assist Nurse Practitioners in opening successful clinics across the United States.

Her educational background started at Wake Technical Community College in Raleigh, North Carolina. She obtained an Associate Degree in Nursing in December 2005. In 2011, she earned her Bachelor's Degree in Nursing from the Queen's

University of Charlotte in Charlotte, North Carolina. She furthered her education at the University of Texas in Arlington, where she obtained a Master's Degree in Nursing with a specialization in Psychiatry in 2015. In 2019, she completed a Doctorate in Nursing Practice. Dr. Olloh was inducted into the Nursing Honor Society while obtaining her Bachelor's and Master's degree.

If you are struggling with your calling in Nursing or any other field? You are not sure if a career in Nursing is right for you? Or you are already a Nurse Practitioner but need some direction with your calling, please contact Dr. Christy Olloh via email: called2BARN@gmail.com

For further information about Dr. Christy Olloh, visit the following websites:

https://www.mcpgpsychiatry.com

https://called2banurse.com

Reigning In Your Passion: Finding Your PATH As An Entrepreneur

By: Temika N. Younger, MSN-Ed, RN

Nursing: A Matter of the Heart

I am a nurse first. I have always been a "nurse". Even before I was licensed, I was a nurse. Being a nurse is a matter of the heart.

No matter what other vocation or area I have focused on, I have always been a caregiver first. I grew up with a great family and loved them all dearly, but I lived mostly with my grandmother who kept me when my mom went back to work. My mother works in the health care profession also. I was taught very early on how to care for other people. I was essentially always around people who were caring for others. Whether it was in the facilities that my mom and aunt worked for, or with my grandmother who always had children around and was always caring for someone. She was a sought-after foster mother in our county and was noted to have taken care of as many as 100 children in her home over a twenty-year span. When I was a toddler, my grandmother had the 24/7 responsibility of taking care of my sweet cousin Stevie, who developed cerebral palsy as an infant. He required total care and even had a gastrostomy tube that he was fed through around the clock. I learned very early in life how to take care of him. I learned how to prevent muscle contractures and atrophy and how to care for a PEG tube from my grandmother who had only an 8th grade education, yet was one of the smartest people I have ever met. She had never had any formal training as a nurse and was not taught these skills in a school, but she just knew what to do. She took care of everyone that came through her home in some way, shape or form. Some she took care of in more physical ways, like Stevie, and others on a more emotional and mental level. She taught me how to do the same. She groomed me to be a caregiver. So, I knew from the beginning that I was on the PATH to becoming a nurse.

Preparation for Nursing

Most will not believe this now, but I was a very shy child. I had a few good friends, but I really was not bold enough to talk to people. When someone spoke to me, I would often tuck my head and speak very softly. Surprisingly though, I had no issue with singing in front of audiences. I sang solos at church almost every Sunday without any fear. Speaking, however, was a separate issue. Since I knew that ultimately I wanted to be a nurse and I knew I would need to learn to get over my fear of talking to people, I decided in my sophomore year of high school to take a drama course. I was scared and extremely nervous, but my teacher was very supportive and welcoming when I decided to join. Transitioning from being on the field in Marching band to the center stage was certainly an uncomfortable change. There was comfort in being dressed in a uniform on a field with 40 other people where I would not be seen readily. A stage, where I would be front and center and certainly seen and heard by all in attendance, was a "field" that I was not sure I was ready for. However, once I started, I became very content playing the roles I was given. So much so, that I excelled in Drama/Forensics competition and won several awards. It was exciting to me to close my eyes and pretend to be someone else and have people enjoy the performance given. After achieving that, I was ready to train to be a nurse.

I graduated high school with honors and was ready to embark on my nursing school journey. I had been accepted into many colleges, but had selected a college only an hour away from home as my choice. I was excited to get started on my education to become a nurse. Everything was going as expected in my first year. I was making friends, succeeding in my studies and adjusting well to this new experience, until the college decided to drop their nursing program that same year. I was automatically placed in the Physical Therapy program. I was shocked and confused at the same time. After seeing the change in majors, I thought about it for a couple of weeks, wondering whether I should just continue in the PT program. I was doing well at this school and had made friends, so maybe I would just stay. That idea would never settle in my spirit as the right decision. So I finally went to my counselor and explained that I wanted nursing, not physical therapy, but she stated that her hands were tied. I was not sure now what my options were, however, I knew it was not what I had been called to do, and decided that I needed to find another route. I left that school on a quest to find the new PATH that I would need to take, in order to continue nursing studies. While searching for a school, I decided to start working.

Since my family had worked in nursing homes for as long as I could remember, I decided maybe that would be an option for me while finding a new school to enroll in. My mom helped me get a job at the facility she worked for. I was given the title of ancillary aide, which simply meant that I would fill ice pitchers, make beds and distribute meal trays to the residents. I figured that this would give me the opportunity to get a taste of real caregiving. I thoroughly enjoyed this job, as I was able to get to know the residents and bring smiles to their faces. Growing up with my grandmother, I had a great appreciation for the geriatric population and what they had to offer to the world. I loved it so much that the management convinced me to take the Nurse Aide Course so that I could be certified as a nurse's aide and do higher level duties than I could as an ancillary aide. Soon after I enrolled in the course, I was accepted into a nursing program in my hometown and I was ecstatic! I became a Certified Nursing Assistant (CNA) right before starting this new nursing program and was able to work full-time throughout the period I was in nursing school. In 3 years,

I officially became a Registered Nurse. This was my PATH for now.

Passion for Education:

In my first two years of nursing, I was given the opportunity to change the course of my career. I had no clue that this PATH would ever be a part of my life. In the long-term care establishment I worked in, I was asked to assist in forming the Nurse Aide Training Program at the facility. The facility was in a very small town and finding employees that were Certified Nursing Assistants was very difficult. The management thought it best to recruit and train interested parties in-house. I, along with two other nurses, were sent to training to learn how to teach a CNA course. Wait, they wanted me to TEACH?! Me? The shy girl who barely talked to people before taking a drama class in high school. You want me to teach the class? I was not sure what I was getting myself into. I had been a CNA for 3 years prior to becoming a nurse and I was sure that my mom, along with all my other CNA coworkers taught me well during that time. At barely 22 years old, could I do this? Maybe I could do it. Then my optimism kicked in. I could do this! From the moment I stepped into that classroom, I knew! I cannot explain the feeling, but I sensed in my spirit a passion for this. It felt natural, easy; just right. I could not wait to get to work to teach on the days that I was assigned to. It felt so good to give back in this way. It felt great to be able to motivate students and see them achieve things they did not think they could. It was so rewarding that I decided to start looking for many more opportunities to teach. I did quite a bit of part-time teaching over the next few years to cure this itch to teach. I taught at a college for 5 years and got a chance to explore my passion even further. At times, I was teaching individuals that were my grandmother's age, but despite my young age, the mutual respect we had for each other was amazing. There were so many success stories that came

61

out of that opportunity. I believe that each of those students could feel the love I had for them. Some of them still stay in contact with me to this very day. I will never forget the day that my boss came and sat in on my class. I was somewhat nervous, wondering why he was auditing my class. He later told me that he had been hearing so many students talk about how much they enjoyed my classes that he needed to see for himself. He felt that often when students rave over a teacher, that instructor may be too easy and that may be the reason why the students are so fond of that teacher. He jokingly said, "I thought you might be giving A's for putting their names on the test". I was relieved to hear that after he sat in the class, he better understood why the students liked my style. Even in a class of twenty plus students, he felt like he was the only one in the room when I was teaching, as if I was "teaching directly to him," he stated. I was flattered. I did not necessarily think I was doing anything special. I truly just enjoyed pouring into these students and giving them what others had given me over the years. It was simply a joy to be in the presence of so many wonderful people who really wanted to learn more and excel further. The college recognized me at the state level as instructor of the year, and I will never forget that great honor. This had undoubtedly become my passion! I had found my PATH!

On the Road to Entrepreneurship

Before 2005, I had never even thought about being an entrepreneur. I thought I had found my ultimate passion and had just planned to further that. However, I was given an opportunity in 2005 that would begin to change my mindset in that area. You may remember that nurse aide training was the class that ignited my fire for teaching, so that particular training was always close to my heart. In 2005, I then embarked on a journey to manage a health care training program. I remember the first time I met with my new boss there. After I was hired, I had seen the resumes of the other nurses that applied for the job, and I did not feel qualified after seeing the credentials they all had. So, I asked him what made them choose me for that job. I will never forget what he said. He exclaimed, "The God in me connected with the God in you and I knew you were the right choice." He then went on to say that he was grooming me for business ownership one day. As I sat there with my mouth opened wide, I said, "Me? What do you mean? I have never thought of owning a business," and I chuckled. He said, "I see it in you". That day was a turning point for me.

This health care training "school" initially only included nurse aide training. We worked tirelessly to add programs to this school and to grow it to a higher level. After almost 9 years, we had expanded to have not only multiple nurse aide trainings, but we also had medication aide, personal care aide and CPR trainings. I had the pleasure of overseeing about 15 nurses who were teaching these courses in 3 different cities in the state of Virginia. This was undeniably the start of great things. This is when I started to feel that I was being pulled into entrepreneurship. I had a strong desire to help others who were interested in education and wanted to help those individuals evolve in this area of nursing. I decided I would start a small business to consult with people who wanted to open training programs to teach nurse aides or medication aides. I wanted the name to be special, so after praying about it, I decided that I wanted my grandmother to be a part of it. I chose to use her initials as a part of the business name. I called it Empowering Health Care Professionals (EHP) Training Consultants. The business started as just a way to give back to others and give assistance to someone else in achieving their goals. EHP Training Consultants was up and running, and we were able to help a few nurses get started in the first couple of years. But God was tugging on my heart to dream bigger and to go after something even greater. The goal was to help others find the PATH they were seeking, and I needed to find a way to assist more people. I had learned a great deal throughout the decade and had a strong desire to pass that knowledge on to others. I was reminded of a lady, Christine Stacy, whom I met in 2000 and the conversation I had with her at that time, and I felt an urge to call her. It took me a few months to make the call because I was afraid of what this next step would lead to. However, I put aside my anxiety and finally called her. We set up a meeting and things began to become clearer. I was beginning to see where this PATH could potentially lead me. More schooling was the next step. I had been doing the job of a Masters Prepared Nurse for years without the title, and I thought this would be a great time to pursue the degree so that once I stepped out, I would have not only the experience, but also the credentials to do so. I started a full-time online Master of Science in Nursing program within a couple of months. I was serious about this PATH but could not stop there. I had to make some hard decisions because that tugging on my heart would not cease, and my spirit was not settled. I had to follow God's leading. So, I did. It was difficult, but I did! After careful consideration, I put in my 30-day notice at my then current full-time job and started on my quest toward this new PATH that I believed God was pushing me to. I was scared. I prayed, a lot! This was a huge step! However, I realized that fear was normal. Anytime you step out into the unknown, fear will be present. But we cannot let fear consume us or keep us from accomplishing our goals. My New PATH was waiting!

New Path Realized

I was given the opportunity to work with a private education company that was owned by Mrs. Stacy. When she hired me, I remember her specifically saying, "I think you may be the reason I retire." Even though she did not know me very well, the trust and hope she had for me was so inspiring. It motivated me to push even harder. I had been managing training programs and training other nurses to teach these programs for many years, so this job was perfect for me. In this job, my responsibility was to conduct train-the-trainer courses for nurses wanting to teach medication aide trainings. Other train-the-trainer courses were offered as well, but my main responsibility was the training for those nurses in medication aide courses. I was in heaven! What an awesome opportunity! With this chance, I would be able to share the tricks of the trade with other nurses who presently had the same goals that I had when I was starting my career in education. This was my dream, and I had been given the chance to walk in it. I continued to develop EHP Training Consultants as well and since it was growing, we became an LLC. I was hired by several clients all across the state. Many of them wanted me to assist with applications and policies. The clients I have worked with have been able to start successful personal care aide, nurse aide and medication aide training programs. Running successful training programs was my strength, so I was able to give some guidance to them. I even had the opportunity to help clients write their policies for their training programs as well as for the startup of a group home. In 2016, I was able to buy Mrs. Stacy's business. What she had spoken in 2013 came true. She was able to retire. Virginia Adult Care Education LLC (VACE) became my company as well and is a subsidiary of EHP Training Consultants. I had yet another PATH.

My Path: My Businesses

Currently, my businesses, VACE and EHP Training Consultants, work as a collaborative unit. These businesses are all about empowering nurses and other health care professionals through education. We offer several training opportunities for nurses, nurse managers, long term care administrators, assisted living administrators and other health care professionals. We offer 1) Train the trainer courses for nurses who want to teach Nurse Aide (CNA) training 2) Train the Trainer courses for nurses who want to teach Medication Aide training 3) Train the Trainer courses for nurses who want to teach a 40 hour direct care staff training/personal care aide training 4) Developing the Individualized Service Plan (ISP) Training and 5) Administrator/Manager trainings. Our newest course is a training that focuses on helping individuals start their own nurse aide (CNA) or Medication Aide training programs. The program is simply called, "How to Start Your Own Training Business". I was the first in our state to write a program such as this. In it, I share all that I know regarding training businesses. After 20 years of teaching these entry level programs, I believe that I have some valuable information to share. I walk the trainees through necessary steps to opening a business such as this, as well as providing sample policies and assistance with completion of applications to become approved training programs. All our trainings are accredited through a national accrediting body and therefore, all our trainings offer CEU's. Your new PATH can be potentially found in one of these trainings.

Face Your Fear: Find Your Path

Is business ownership for you? Well, first, have you thought about the PATH you want to take? That is the first step. There are so many areas of opportunity as a nurse entrepreneur. Do not choose your PATH based on the wrong assumptions. Do not choose your PATH based on how much money you think you will make. Search for the area that makes you happiest. Search for the topic that causes you to light up when you speak about it. Search for the subject that you get excited about researching and learning more about. Search for the thing that makes getting up to do it easy. Search for the PATH that brings you joy. The money will come. One part of choosing your right PATH is knowing yourself and knowing your strengths. What motivates you? What are you willing to risk? What will you do to be successful? Some element of fear is normal. Whenever you are embarking on something new or uncomfortable, there will always be some anxiety associated with it. However, once you find your PATH, things will start to fall into place. I knew I had found my PATH the first day I stepped into the classroom. I knew that it made my heart happy to see students excel. I knew that I wanted to reach the unreachable student and help them believe in themselves. The realization was easy. However, it took me some years to develop my God-given talent into a profitable skill. It will take time. Do not give up! Be patient with yourself, but also know that you must put in the work. The passion you have for your PATH will propel you forward, but gaining knowledge will steer you in the right direction. I had to educate myself by going to seminars. I had to listen to people who

66

were doing what I wanted to do. These mentors were eager to share with me and help me learn but I had to be a willing vessel. One of the biggest pieces of advice I give to the clients I work with is to listen. I am willing to share my experiences with them. In the area of nurse education and the development of training programs, I have made some mistakes. However, I am willing to be transparent and share those errors so that someone else does not have to go through that same thing. Metaphorically, if I know that the stove is hot, I will let you know not to touch it. This is the way I feel about business. I am willing to tell you my mishaps, so you do not have to make the same ones. So, listen! Secondly, I would encourage nurses to keep their day job until their business can sustain itself. As you have already read, I opened my business as a side hustle while I was still working my full-time job. I worked that business for 3 years before quitting my full-time job. There were some long nights and early mornings, but it was worth it. I think it prepared me for the real world of business ownership. Thirdly, find your PATH but start off with a narrow PATH. With that I mean, find your niche and stay within that when the business first starts. You will have time to broaden that later, but you should perfect your primary niche first before branching off into other areas. Lastly, keep a positive outlook. I am a firm believer that what you believe will be, and what you speak will be. Speak life over your business PATH. Speak what you want to see, not what you see currently. It is not about what you see. It is about what you believe you can achieve. I know it sounds cliché, but you truly have whatsoever you believe in your mind. If you need to keep a list of positive affirmations where you can see them, do it. Repeat them often. Faith is what has carried me through this venture, and it can carry you too. Entrepreneurship is not for the faint of heart. This is twenty-four hours a day, seven days a week, no sick leave, no PTO. But, it is worth every hour you spend to make it happen. Now, go discover your PATH and achieve your dream!

About The Author

Temika N. Younger has been in the health care field for over 2 decades. She received her registered nursing education at Centra College of Nursing (Formerly Lynchburg General School of Nursing). She later earned her Master of Science in Nursing Education from Lynchburg College. She has progressively 'risen through the ranks' of her chosen profession. Her health care career began as a certified nurse aide (CNA) during her college years. As a registered nurse, she has worked in many areas of long-term care. Temika has held positions such as Nursing Supervisor, MDS Coordinator (local and regional) and Assistant Director of Nursing. It was in her position as Nurse Educator that she discovered her talent for and love of teaching caregivers how to provide better care. Having her start as a CNA, Temika understands the art of caregiving and how important it is to be a well-trained, and competent care provider. Her mantra is "reach them to teach them." She continuously strives to personally meet each student where they are and help them to excel to greater heights. Temika continued to evolve in the area of education and has taught various college level courses such as medical terminology, pharmacology, anatomy and physiology for several years. During that time, she received awards as statewide instructor of the year of that college system. Temika's love for teaching is evident in every class she presents. She is enthusiastic and her training programs are pertinent and enjoyable. She started Empowering Health Care Professionals Training Consultants LLC in 2010 and later added, Virginia Adult Care Education LLC; a prosperous business that trains nurses and other health care professionals across the state of Virginia. In the few short years that she has owned the company, she has taken the organization to new heights. Nurses come from far and near just to sit under Temika's passionate, thought provoking training. Nurses all over the state can attribute their success in their programs partly to the great training they have received under Temika's leadership. She truly has a heart for healthcare. Operating in her God-given passion, her gift has made room for her. Proverbs 18:16.

If you are interested in teaching entry level health care courses or if you desire to start a training business, Temika can help.

To Contact Temika Younger:

Email: temika@vacetraining.com

Facebook: Virginia Adult Care Education

Website: www.vacetraining.com

The Trap House Chronicles

By: Christmas Spencer, LPN

Good morning, good evening, hell good afternoon. Let me ever so politely introduce myself to you. My name is Claudia Spencer, but everyone calls me Christmas, Missionary of the Baptist Church. I want you to sit back, relax, and sip on this tea. Please allow me to enter your mind, and let us explore this rewind, back into my very own timeline. This jaw dropping, shenanigans central reflects the best and worst in humanity. What is right is wrong, and what is wrong is right.

Now that I have your attention, let's proceed down this ghetto ass yellow brick road. Please take a glimpse into my humble beginnings, starting straight out of the hood. I proudly hail from the projects in Brooklyn, New York. Baby ain't nothing like it, growing up in Brownsville and East New York. This area is fondly known as "killa dilla." My mom was an old school type of mother. She was an extremely proud, beautiful, brick house black woman. She was as militant as an old battle ax general, quick on her feet but even faster with her hands. If you rolled your eyes, your neck or stomped your feet, your happy ass got tore up. Momma did not give a hoot who was there or what you were doing; do not let that night streetlight catch you after dark. The shoe, belt or whatever, she had in her hands was waiting for your little fast ass. You got the hollering before the belt, or the wet dish rag could even land on your backside. Raising kids in that environment was tough and I still wonder to this day, how she did it. Just like the desert, living in the hood became a very bleak, harsh, unforgiving, and inhospitable environment. You learn from an early age, survival of the fittest. The rate of succeeding was dismal and poor. I can clearly remember, the pungent smell of days old piss in the elevators and back staircases. We would see the junkies on the corner, completely strung out. They would be in a semi-stupor, bending but never

70

falling to the ground. They would nod, and drool from the mouth with a ragged cigarette drooping from their mouths.

Momma would quickly gather us up and walk past them. Her head was elevated and her heels never missed beat on that broken concrete pavement. I often wonder what was more broken, the junkies on the corner or the crumble concrete on the streets. Momma would look sternly at those lost souls; her ice pick or straight razor was never too far from those deadly hands.

Momma restricted our movements like vice grips. Basically, your ass never got too far that she could not get to you. Hell, we were afraid of our own shadows. Now, my childhood was not all gloom and doom. I missed Sunday dinners, and that homemade old fashion cake, where we would fight to lick the spoon and bowl. The music was the best ever, and Disco was in. You knew who was in love, or who just broke up, by the music they were playing. Back then the music had true meaning, with love and happiness and most importantly, respect. You can shake your groove thing without having your jewels hanging out. But I want to touch on the Baptist church for just a brief moment or two. On the blessed Sabbath day, getting your hair straightened with that hot comb. Jesus, if you moved or flinched, your ass just got burnt plus cussed out. Lord have mercy. We had to put on our Sunday best drawers, stockings and you better not put a hole in that damn thing either, not a scratch up your black patten leather shoes. My aunties Mother Blake and Sister Marylou were the head of the Usher Board. Many times, we would get hit by the funeral home prayer fans. Honey, if you laughed, guess what? your ass got tore up too. But hold up, hold up, if you tried to get smart, then that tree switch cleared the whole bench. Then you got a can of whoop ass from momma for showing out in church. Believe it or not I missed those carefree days.

The child in me thought my momma was the meanest, shortest black woman in America. However, the woman that is within me could literally kiss the very ground that those high heels walked on in that broken concrete jungle. She had sacrificed everything for us, to be better than the next generation. After all we were considered the Jefferson's of the projects. Momma taught us to get a good education, find a good job, retire and get your pension. However, we were never taught to have our own businesses.

Thank you for allowing me to take that brief trip down memory lane. My heart is filled with happiness and the pain of that little girl's dreams. Just maybe some of you all can identify with me. I pretty much followed my mother's blueprints and mindset most of my adult life. This was both a blessing and a curse at the same time. When I reflect upon that mindset, like Eddie Kendrick, would say, "Baby you need a change of mind."

My high school years were mostly uneventful. My mom switched me back into a female catholic school. There were a bunch of haters, with mean girl mentality. I represented my hood proudly and they left my happy ass alone. When people discover you are from Brownsville, East New York, they would generally scurry out of your way, like rats trying to escape the mouse traps. I showed my haters; I was one of the speakers of my graduating class. I was deemed the new clap black kid. My biggest regret was not going to prom, but life still goes on.

College years were a blur in my rearview window. Chile let freedom rang. In my case it rang a little too damn much. I did not have my momma in my shadow and you could not tell me nothing. I truly lived for the moment, but not for the future. Jack Daniels was my best friend and Johnny Walker Black a very close second. Nonetheless, you can party that Saturday night, but you had to get your ass up drunk or sober to be in church. Lord have mercy, at least I made it before the benediction. My decisions were poor and the regrets at the time were few. But in my youthful days the levels of arrogance and ignorance were great. Momma used to say, "you have issued a check that your ass can't cash."

Only, by the grace of God was I able to get a bachelor's degree in political science. Have you all heard of the old saying, "a hard head makes for a soft ass?" I was flying high in the friendly skies, without ever leaving the ground. I was with people that I had no business with, who came with problems and hidden agendas. Focusing on law school was not an option at that time. Ignorantly, shrugging my shoulders, I settled for less. As a New York City Probation Officer, I had a hint of clout. But I quickly got burnt out with a caseload of over 218 people. My God, that was a harshly learned lesson of the cruelty against humanity. The criminals were often victims themselves.

I returned back home pregnant with no one but my momma holding and supporting me. Fast forward I gave birth to my oldest daughter, Ms. Lacey, who was a blessing because she redirected and gave me a meaningful purpose in my young life. Still trying to find my purpose, I headed south. What in the hell was I thinking? If you make your bed hard, you got to lay in it. Folks that Bitch was too damn hard. I wallowed in exile at my own pity party.

Looking back through the windowpane of my past, I often wondered what the hell I was thinking about becoming a nurse. This seed was planted a long time ago. During my scoliosis surgery, I remembered this big proud black momma bear of a nurse named Ms. Gloria. She was very stout and shaped like a linebacker, but had the bedside manner of a guardian angel. She touched something within me during that painful tumultuous hospitalization. I will never forget as a teenager, she stood up to this world's renowned spinal surgeon, Dr. Michael Neuwirth about my plan of care.

My mind was very foggy and my body was racked with pain. I literally felt a thousand and one needles buried deep into my spinal nerve endings. She argued and advocated regarding my pain medications. I went from a morphine drip to Tylenol #3 without any titrating dosage. I distinctly remembered the tears rolling down my face. I was too weak to yell out, my face twisted up in pure unadulterated pain. Bedsides, my militant mom, she was my hero. Here, a complete stranger, fighting like hell for me, to get my pain management under control. Finally, she took the bull by the horns and got the order to adjust the pain medications and to also update my plan of care.

I survived that awful recovery period of learning how to walk, eat, and talk again. This giant of a woman always embraced me like a protective security blanket on a cold winter night. It's been over 30 years, since I last saw my momma bear Nurse Gloria. But warm memories, and that advocating spirit attached to my subconscious mindset. Title did not matter, but what is best for the patient, that's what it is all about. Slowly the seed of becoming a nurse started smothering like a moth to a flame.

I became stagnant and set in my rebellious ways. Life was good and decisions were bad. Before you knew it, everything you had worked for literally disappeared in front of you. Where are all my friends? Come to find out once the glitz, glamour and money runs out, Bitch you are on your own.

Life began to pass me. My self-esteem was eroded and shot straight to hell. But I was raised by a praying momma. I had a family to feed, and they were depending on me. I was determined to succeed at any cost.

When I look back, and see what the Lord has brought me threw, both seen and unseen dangers. I got to shout and give him praise. Because, when I did not have a door to open, hallelujah, he blew the damn door wide open. When I needed shelter in the midst of that storm, his very presence comforted me late in that midnight hour. Lord, have mercy I have to move on but I just had to reflect on his goodness and his mercy. This is why I am standing in front of you all telling this part of my journey. God is not a myth, but is he ever so real. You have to try and know him for yourself, to know what I am talking about.

Nursing school challenged me from the very beginning. You had to be regimented and determined like a dog fighting over a bone. You really did not have time for yourself or your family. Due to the extreme stressors of studying, clinicals and exams, relationships were often broken. Unfortunately, friendships were destroyed. Humbly speaking, nursing school was much worse than given birth or getting teeth pulled from a dentist. In retrospect, nursing school was worth every blood, sweat and tears.

Looking back over my nursing career, there were many ebbs and flows in my bumpy journey to no man's land. I knew I was smart enough but the million-dollar question was "did I have what it would take to stay the course?" Nursing school itself was harsh, but being on the clinical floor was worse. We all first started with big dreams and aspirations of the new modern nurse nightingale. Hair and nails were well manicured, not a strand out of place. Bright shining faces so eager to learn and to impress our peers and managers. Baby here comes the tsunami tidal waves knocking everything and everyone off of their feet. The fresh dewy makeup now looked like a caked up hot mess. The hair resembled a bad wig or even better like an unkempt mop. I soon wondered what in the hell did I get my happy ass into. Hold up wait a minute, I did not sign up for this crap. Once again innocence was lost within a blink of an eye.

I had to quickly adapt; only the strong survive. The sacrifices were all too painful but absolutely necessary. I felt like an island alone in a very unfriendly and barren land. Miserable, lonely and caught out on a limb, my momma was lifeline and my daughter my anchor. Failure was not an option. My mind quickly left the fairytale phase and went straight into beast mode. Brooklyn born, Brooklyn raised, I had to endure and finish this race.

Like a moth to a flame, you crashed and burned. Hands shaking, palms sweating and nerves just unraveling. Life itself became a box of chocolates. You never knew what the next day was going to bring. Once I had graduated, I became that black nurse with the big butt in that white crisp uniform and white cap. That cap had a life of its own, it would at times slide to the side or lean back like Fat Joe. Nonetheless, I wore it with grace and dignity. The boost in salary was both a blessing and a curse at the same time. For so long I had done without, and the money burnt like a hole in my pocket. I had a new jack swing in my talk and walk. Hell, before I knew it, I was sponsoring everybody's children. Quick, someone, get the violin out and the sob stories kept on rolling. Foolish me, trying to help and wearing my heart on my sleeves. Always giving but never taking.

The years and tears eventually merged with each other. Here I was, pregnant and broke. I could not believe this growing fact in my stomach. Oh my God, I have not been pregnant in over 10 years. I looked in the mirror and I did not even recognize myself. How did I get here? I checked my bank account and it was dry and as barren as the Sahara Desert. I looked up most of the people I had helped along the way and I really could not find anybody. Where were all my friends? Harsh reality quickly set in, baby girl you are on your own.

I had to man up and put my baby girl panties on. I worked Baylor shift at a local nursing home. The locals affectionately call it the La Britt. Every month there was chaos and pure pandemonium. We had to get the health department to do all of our TB screening. Somehow, a new admit had active TB and no one had an idea why he was admitted to that facility. Never mind that he had already been there a total of 3 weeks. Jesus, what a mess. Then there was the bed bugs revolution. It was so deeply infested that Life safety threatened to shut the damn building down. Finally, I got tired of the circus atmosphere and went agency. Now, why and the hell did I do that. Talking about going from the frying pan into the fire. The bigger my belly got, the stronger I sharpened my survival skills in nursing. I became the black nurse version of the late great Kenny Rogers. You got to know when to hold them. Know when to fold them, know when to walk away, and know when to run. You better count your money when you are sitting at the table and the dealing is done.

I had always loved that song, but I had no idea, how those very words would literally shape and change my mindset. I was no longer the pushover. I pushed back and climbed myself out of that hole. Or so I thought. Sometimes old habits are hard to get rid of. Now I had two mouths to feed that were solely depending on me. My second daughter Pepperose gave me a total of 54 stitches in my vaginal area. She was the gift that keeps on giving. I promised myself no more.

Her dad was more absent than present. His demands and behavior were unacceptable and damn near unforgiveable.

Baby, this time I had to put my girdle on in addition to my big girl drawers on. Oh, hell no, no more lies, deceptions, half baked, half ass truths. Enough was enough. I could not go down this yellow brick road. My oldest daughter was a God send and I went back to work only 2 weeks after giving birth. I could distinctively remember, the pain of pushing that heavy med cart, blood pooling and filling up my double pads. I would go to the bathroom, clean myself up, take some Motrin 800 mg and just cry in silence. My gait was extremely poor and my body was bent over in unrelenting pain. My mind wondered how our ancestors birthed babies and were back in the field the next day. This factual statement still boggles my mind. Lord, I cried my body is not built for this. I thought about my children and their future. Once again failure was not an option. I felt a spiritual presence cloak and calm my soul, giving me the strength to endure and finish the race.

I have learned the hard way that time does not stand still for nobody. My children were getting older and requiring much more than one salary could afford. Thus, my journey into the nursing home chaos and madness. I began to work two jobs to overly compensate my kids, because they did not have a suitable father figure in their lives. Materialistic things such as the latest gadgets, clothes or whatnot, the cost did not matter. I am going to trap for this money come hell or high water. And somehow along the way, I lost a sense of humility.

Honey, I was like a female stallion pulling long hours back to back and bringing home decent wages in the deep south. But the more I worked, I saw things that bothered my very core, as a woman, as a mother, and as a fellow human being. This is where I get a huge dose of reality and most Welcome to the wonderful world of agency. You are thrown to the wolves when you get your assignment. I quickly realized it was a mental challenge of do or die. Guess what? I was raised by a strong black woman and I refused to run or hide. My mind was racing, nerves were shot and I just wanted to fart or throw up. But neither of the above happened. I raised my chin, my back was rim rod straight, my eyes were as cold as ice. I said to my young self, let's get it lets go.

Lord have mercy, there were no supplies, no linen, no staff to properly assist you with any damn thing. I got report from a very cranky, overworked and underpaid season nurse. She literally threw the keys my way with the report sheet and yelled good luck, while slamming the med room door. I jumped up and snatched the door handle from her dry, dull, dusty ashy hands. I told her a line from color purple, "all my life I had to fight." Believe you me, I got her undivided attention then. Now let's start this conversation all over again. She tried to be nice then. Folks, I learned the hard way once someone shows you their true colors, act accordingly, and handle them with a long wooden spoon.

I should have known that this was the beginning of my descent into hell. I kept telling and convincing myself that I could change the narrative of the dismal work conditions in the nursing home. Who in the hell left the gates open because the devil has run amuck and stolen the joy out of true bedside nursing? It was extremely hard to decipher who was your friend or enemy. You could not trust anyone but God and your dollar.

Baby, go and get that second drank of brew because you are going to need it. Believe you me, it ain't safe in these streets and extremely dangerous at times in the nursing homes, that we called the Trap House. It is like that song, Welcome to The Hotel California; you can check out, but you can never leave. Clocking in and out of some of these hell holes, you pray every day that your nursing license is protected like Allstate.

The nursing home industry is like a runaway train with no brakes. The staffing ratio is piss poor, and the overall care is subpar. There are few resources and a high demand to produce and yield good results. On any given day you will have one nurse to 40 plus patients, not counting new admissions. You are expected to pass meds, help feed, answer call lights, and do your scheduled treatments, all within an 8-12-hour time period. Please do not forget to chart. Their care tracker states every 2 hours that a patient was turned and repositioned or briefs were changed. We know that this was a bold, bald faced lie. There is no way on this earth that one can take care of 30 plus people on one shift. This is fraud at its best.

You have to borrow supplies because the company refused to buy decent quality items that are required for care. Many times, residents did not get properly fed or changed because there was no staff. Skin breakdown and bed sores are real. These areas are often infected with bacteria and pus, and sometimes maggots. Yes, I said maggots; there are always flies and gnats in patients' rooms and the nasty soil utility rooms. Now, do not forget the bedbugs and scabies, due to the lack of cleanliness. But these facilities have the base lying people in management to spin another tale. Once again, when state comes across those doors, they pass with flying colors. There have been times, residents were found outside the facility turned upside down in a ditch, or roaming in the local hood. Those incidents never got reported. The demographics have changed to a younger set of residents who are victims of car accidents or gunshot wounds. They are often demanding and will have drugs and alcohol in their systems. Question, if they do not go out of the facility, which staff members are bringing it into the facility? Nobody seems to know. Nurses continued to steal narcotics like water flowing out of a facet. They are rarely arrested but they opt out to resign. Sad but true.

The violence had increased, the physicians had cut down on their psychotropic medications, per pharmacy recommendations. These awful decisions make it 10 times harder on staff to care for that resident. Often, aggressive and combative behaviors are getting out of hand. Management just wants to keep bodies in the building to keep their census up. State comes in the building for complaints and annual survey. Now there are staff tripping over each other and the lies that we are never short staffed. REALLY, the lies you tell. Some way or another the complaints are rarely substantiated and the survey is favorable. I wonder in the back of my mind how much hush money was exchanged.

Taking care of morbid obese people without the proper equipment or staff is beyond greed. You got residents falling out of the Hoyer lift, unexplained deep tissue wounds. Showers not given mostly due to lack of staffing. No matter how many of us old school nurses hold a facility down, we are never recognized. Most of us get looked over for promotions, or pay raise. If you ask too many questions, or advocating for your residents, all of a sudden get terminated. The list of mismanagement goes on into the dismal abyss.

I thought that I could make a viable, valuable difference. I had the years of experience in, attendance good, attitude humble. Guess what I was often denied many positions? The most famous line: only a RN can work in that slot. Wait a damn minute, I have been doing this particular job as an LPN for years. The excuses were so lame and they could not quite look my way. Frustration and despair grew. I tried getting my RN credentials, but the hands of time were against me.

Further sinking into a black hole of depression, I asked God to send me the right people to help me help myself. I took a leap of faith, I did not know when or how, but I knew a change was going to come. Lord, who are these people? He told me in a dream, you will know them when you see them. My spirit was touched and I knew in my heart of hearts a change was here. This was and is my exodus out of the land of Egypt. Lord have mercy I am about to be delivered out of the nursing home trap house.

People thought I was crazy. But for those who knew the word by the word informed me that my blessing was here. True story, I was on Facebook and came across black nurses' rock and black nurses' entrepreneur groups. I started scrolling down and came across both Tamara Neely and Chanelle Washington post. My spirit instantly connected, and know I had my answer. These 2 ladies were my golden ticket out of the trap house. I reached out and both ladies were honest, humble and more than willing to extend a helping hand. Nothing in this life is free, however, the cost and fees were doable. The classes, webinars and hands-on were also invaluable. There are several things that stood out with these ladies. They are still accessible even though that particular set of classes has ended. But most importantly, they are loaves of fisherman. They will feed you, but also teach you how to feed yourself. My mindset was forever changed.

The last couple of months flew by like a whirl wind. I was taught to get a business bank account, registered my business as an LLC in the Carolinas. My revisions were sent back to the state government and I am just one stone away from getting my nonmedical home care license. I am government contract ready. I was so ambitious that I took a course in body contouring with Keema and I was hooked. Wow, I am starting 2 businesses at the same time. My hopes and dreams were finally coming true. My spirit was dancing to its own drumbeat. I was on cloud nine, flying high in the friendly skies, without ever leaving the ground. Finally, I got a seat at the table, that God had created just for me. No longer would I have to ask for permission to be included and seated at that nursing home trap house table. Nurse boss nation here I come.

Preparing for my grand opening for Everyday Life Home Care Services and Indigoblu Contouring and Body Studio. I had already secured an office space outside of the Charlotte, North Carolina. I

took great pride in ordering most of my equipment from overseas for my opening event. Baby, I trapped those nursing homes shifts to get my business up and running. Body tired, back, hip and knee all out of alignment, and to add insult to injury, my hemorrhoids dropped down. Lord have mercy I am so close, I can feel it, touch it and taste it. What God has for you is just for you. No man, chick, or child can take it away from you. And then you all have not met
CORONAVIRUS.

My world was rocked, and I was stunned. I planned meticulously. I never came up against a virus that was deadly and did not discriminate. The state government shut down everything and everybody. My money was lost and my shipment from overseas delayed. Both the shock and disappointment flowed thru my veins. I walked around in a daze; angry, mad and upset that my apple cart was overturned. Why Lord, I cried. Lost in my own misery, I did not know my left from my right. I reached back to Chanelle and Tamara and Keema. Brainstorming how can you get a business back up and running in the midst of COVID-19. After communicating with my mentors, my spirit experienced a revival. Delayed but not yet denied. That became my go-to slogan. It started like fire shut up in my bones.

Pivoting in midstream to reach my goal of 7 streams of income. Being a proud investor in a medical company and a proud active member of funding the block. Applying to the state of North Carolina to become an independent lab, specializing in COVID-19 testing kits. Independent travel COVID nurse within my nursing home facility. Coming soon to a theatre near you. Indigoblu Self Indulgence line of weight loss super foods products, supplements, coaching, waist trainers, corsets, waist beads and e-books. Wow, in less than 1 year, look at what I have accomplished on a shoestring budget. This includes the 3 Ts, fixing my taxes, teeth and toes. The old saying is true: if you can believe, then you can achieve. Remember, the race is not given to the swift but to those who can endure. And the marathon continues.

About The Author

Christmas Spencer is an aspiring black nurse entrepreneur. She has a bachelor's degree in political science and a diploma in practical nursing.

Christmas is a dedicated License Practical Nurse in the nursing home and rehabilitation industry for over 24 years. She has made it one of her life missions to give comfort and compassionate care to our geriatric population.

Christmas has worked in various nursing positions ranging from a charge nurse, wound care, admissions and discharges, MDS, and hospice palliative care. More recently she travels to medically assist other facility buildings that are COVID-19 positive.

Christmas has stepped up her game and taken her wealth of experience and passion to a nurse boss level. She has answered the call to start her own non-medical home care services that will be directly providing testing for COVID-19.

Her diverse portfolio includes being an investor in startup businesses, retailing body contouring and weight loss products. Christmas' business is currently government-contract ready. She is always on the lookout for bigger and better investment opportunities.

To Contact Christmas Spencer:

Email: indigoblu2407@gmail.com

www.thetraphousechronicles.com

Stepping Into Entrepreneurship

By: April McGraw BSN, RN

My name is April McGraw born in Detroit, Michigan, and growing up all over. I'm blessed to be happily married with two bonus children and three beautiful grandkids. I come from a close knit family that includes my mother, and three sisters -who are my best friends. An adult niece, and a teen nephew. My life is relatively full with caring for my family and running my business. I've been a Nephrology nurse for 18 years. To add to that, I have lived with and coped with two chronic illnesses for over 35 years. I was diagnosed with Lupus at the age of 13, and I started dialysis at the age of 15. Living and coping with those chronic illnesses, enabled me to develop a strong sense of determination, resilience, and empathy as a nurse and person. For most of my nursing career, I have worked in patient care and administration in dialysis, managing the day-to-day operations for a Fortune 500 dialysis company. I can't imagine pursuing any other field of nursing even today.

I didn't always want to be a nurse. Despite my many health challenges with Lupus and End Stage Renal Disease (ESRD), I actually attended college in 1990 at Tennessee State to become an Elementary Education teacher. I quickly realized that this was not the route for me, and I planned to change my major to Social Work as soon as I could. This however, was not a passion of mine, so definitely not the correct route for me. I was clueless as to what to do, so I returned home to California after my first year of college. I took some time trying to figure out exactly what I wanted to be when I grew up, and received my first kidney transplant in1992. I eventually decided to enroll in a Medical

Assistant course to "see if I would like nursing." Little did I know or understand, that those were two totally different worlds.

Unable to secure a job as a Medical Assistant after my move to Mississippi, my former instructor encouraged me to seek jobs as a phlebotomist or x-ray technician, since they were part of my curriculum. I did, and started a job as a phlebotomist in a hospital. This job gave me motivation and willingness to take my education and career further. I loved working in the hospital as a phlebotomist, and secretly admired the nurses that I came in contact with on the med-surg floors, ICU, and other specialty care units. I decided that I wanted to have what I perceived to be sometimes intense interactions with physicians, thoughtful and caring interactions with patients, and to help improve the health of patients as many nurses had done for me over the years as I lived with Lupus and ESRD.

Working as a phlebotomist in a hospital system afforded me the opportunity to attend an 18 month LPN program, and work on the weekends. During that time in my LPN program, my thought process was that I would become an LPN to be able to work and pay my way through a RN program without debt. Well that seemed like a solid plan, and I went for it. It did not quite work out like I planned. I lost that first kidney transplant due to rejection, but continued my LPN studies. However, despite taking the LPN, to ADN, to BSN route, I am an RN today. If I had to do it all over, I would have gone straight into a BSN program. However my journey is my journey and it played out exactly as it was supposed to.

Still not really knowing how I was going to be a nurse while being on dialysis, I just knew that I would make it happen. My nephrologist and nurses would all say that I should come to work in dialysis when I finished my LPN program. I wasn't in the least bit interested in doing that at the time. In my mind, being a dialysis patient and working as a dialysis nurse, would be dialysis overload. I finished my LPN program on time, with minimum issues in regard to my health. I felt accomplished and started working for a state run mental facility with Long Term Care (LTC) services. I did this for a few years while I was still on dialysis and then received my 2nd kidney transplant in 1999. I took the opportunity after receiving my 2nd kidney transplant to return back to school and obtain my RN. So I enrolled in a LPN to RN program which was a year-long, and again I had

my now prior nephrologists and nurses saying that I should work in dialysis. LTC was not my passion, but I was still not interested in working in dialysis as a RN.

As fate would have it, God had different plans despite my interests. I will never forget that day in May 2002, that I took my RN boards. I drove directly to the nearest dialysis facility near my home right afterwards. It just so happened that Rhonda, the manager of the facility, used to be one of my charge nurses that would tell me I should have a career in dialysis as a nurse when I was on dialysis. She said, "April don't apply anywhere else. Between Shirley and I (another one of my nurses while on dialysis) one of us will get you in. Rhonda was true to her word. A week later she reached out to tell me that she had a nurse resignation, and if I was still interested. I said yes! I had not applied anywhere else, and this was the start of my RN career in Nephrology. I lost that second kidney transplant in October 2007, yet I remained a full-time dialysis nurse, and then administrator.

As my career in nursing moved along, and in different roles, I started to realize that I had many marketable skill sets and experiences that allowed me to help healthcare corporations make money while I took care of patients and employees. Those skill sets are valuable and highly sought after in the healthcare world. Entrepreneurship was not on my radar, until the last few years when I started seeing nurses that looked like me step into the nurse entrepreneur space.

The more intrigued I was, the more I would push those thoughts down. Afterall, I had what many would consider a "good job" and earned six figures. The fear of not being able to make enough money to help support my family and live the life I was accustomed to, was another thought in the back of my head. You hear about corporate professionals leaving their six figure jobs every day to start business, spend more time with kids and families, or even travel the world. Why was I different? Was I having unrealistic beliefs about my abilities?

Was I being unrealistic because I was and still am today a dialysis patient? A black woman? Would I be seen as "crazy?" Afterall I was a nurse. I was here in this world to help take care of patients – specifically, dialysis patients- and not run a business. I had all of these thoughts and more that paralyzed me. I had to take a leap of faith. A leap of faith that has proven to be one of the best decisions of my life...besides becoming a nurse.

I am the first college graduate in my family. Despite my own health challenges, I was determined to achieve my degree and be a positive influence and contributor to my community. My nursing experience prepared me for starting my own business in ways that I never would have thought of. For instance, as a chair-side nurse, I learned time management, critical thinking skills, and how to effectively deal with people, which helps me with staying on task and with contract negotiations as an independent business owner. Additionally, as a nurse administrator, I learned how to manage large budgets, as well as making sound financial decisions with money, not only for my company, but also in my personal life.

Working as a dialysis nurse is not easy. You see a lot of sickness and a lot of death, day in and day out. If you're not mindful and careful, you can experience burnout early. The role of nursing has a high incidence of burnout, but certain types of nursing make you more susceptible. At one point I did feel burned out as a dialysis nurse. I hadn't been working in dialysis long and in hindsight, I've come to realize over the course of many years that I wasn't actually burned out, I was grieving. I was grieving the loss of my first marriage and the loss of my maternal grandmother. I was simply trying to find some control in my out-of-control life throughout those significant changes. Thankfully storms don't last forever, and I was able to return to a nurse specialty that would later play a huge part in my career trajectory.

Wanting to become a nurse entrepreneur was a desire that started and grew stronger with each passing year within the last 3 years. I had an overwhelming desire and pull to do more. I felt that since I had been blessed to be able to not only survive but THRIVE with my chronic illnesses, that

I should do more to service this underserved community. I did not act on these thoughts immediately, but each year, the urge became stronger and stronger, until I eventually had to succumb to what was in my heart and ditch the Imposter Syndrome that was threatening to derail my purpose.

Part of the reason I became a nurse entrepreneur was the fact that I could do more for the underserved renal community than I could working a nine-to-five for someone else's company. I identified early on a lot of the issues that were associated with being a dialysis patient, and a lot of the challenges associated with healthcare providers that are tasked with taking care of dialysis patients. Even though there is a lot of education available for dialysis patients, there's still so much more that can be provided.

Consider the fact that there are many times dialysis facilities are understaffed and that the nurses are unable to provide even the basic education to a new or established patient on an ongoing or consistent basis. This lack of nursing staffing can lead to serious deficiencies commonly found during surveys, including medication errors, lack of clinical oversight of patient care technicians, and infection control issues. Nursing shortages also lead to burnouts and increased turnover rates. Insufficient physician involvement in patient care can lead to a lack of quality clinical outcomes and decreased patient experience.

As a vast majority of dialysis patients live in inadequate housing with lack of family support and transportation challenges, socioeconomics disproportionately plague this community of patients. It is important to note that many lack the means or the technology needed to acquire education outside of their dialysis facilities. The absence of CKD education pre-dialysis, typically led to patients being ill-informed, if informed at all, of the different modality choices available to them as a dialysis patient. As a dialysis professional, I saw these challenges play out day after day.

Patient after patient. But I asked myself, "what could I do to add value that PCP's, nephrologists, and dialysis companies could not do in a consistent and meaningful way?

For about a year I constantly thought about what I could do in the nurse entrepreneur space that would help provide a comprehensive CKD program to patients. Continue that education for them as dialysis patients and provide educational support to hospitals, PCP's and nephrologists, assisting them to create an additional layer of patient care outside the traditional thrice-weekly dialysis sessions ordered by the physician. With each passing year, I was getting more comfortable with my mid-level leadership six figure job, and I knew that I needed to be quiet and listen to God.

What I settled on was to become a renal nurse consultant. So on May 4th, 2020 with my exit strategy ready for execution, I resigned from my full-time role as a Home Program Manager, effective June 12th, and never looked back.

As a Home Program Manager, the various barriers for patients considering home dialysis and actually remaining on the therapy are largely known. Lack of motivation, unwillingness, and self-cannulation fears are but a few. For some, the time and financial commitment due to inability to work during home dialysis training is a barrier. For others, the lack of care partner support, and/or burnout, contributes to patients not being able to initiate or remain on a home dialysis therapy. As I continue to note these challenges, I also began to understand what solutions I could offer a healthcare organization to address and/or alleviate these challenges. The problem was that I wanted to implement everyone at the same time!

Some solutions that I noted that could help healthcare organizations overcome these barriers, were to provide adequate pre-dialysis or CKD education in PCP offices. Adequate CKD education goes a long way in setting the mindset of a patient beforehand. It also allows patients to be able to make any improvements or changes in their current lifestyle to either slow down or stop the progression of CKD. Alternatively, prepare them for dialysis or a home therapy as CKD progresses to ESRD. Nurses or PCTs being made available to present to the patients' home to assist with cannulation and home dialysis treatments, would allow nephrologists and dialysis centers to increase their home dialysis penetration rates. Oftentimes the patient simply does not have anyone to support them, and are unable to perform home dialysis therapy without support or assistance despite being interested and willing. Currently Medicare does not reimburse for this service.

This is how iKARE Renal Solutions was born. Born with the idea to consult with PCP's nephrologists and hospitals on ways that they can improve or initiate their CKD education programs. To continue education of dialysis patients in the chronic and hospital acute setting. This is done by providing and implementing CKD and Patient Navigation programs, along with Chronic Care Management programs, to improve quality of care and reduce hospitalization rates of Medicare entitled patients with two or more chronic illnesses. In addition, iKARE Renal Solutions will provide staff assisted home dialysis treatments and support to those who want the ability to perform their dialysis treatments at home.

For healthcare organizations to invest in solutions to their problems, they have to first see it as a problem. They have to see the value in having a solution to the problem, and how that will affect the overall quality of care and patient experience for their patients. Additionally, they must understand and appreciate how these solutions will ultimately affect their organizations' bottom line, and be willing to implement strategies advised by the consultant for improvement of patient care. As a dialysis healthcare professional and patient, I had to believe that healthcare organizations would embrace the opportunity to have a subject matter expert such as myself, to help solve their problems. This was the belief that fueled my desire to do more, to make the decision to step out on faith and do the work that I was destined to do, all while doing what I loved.

Today more than ever, more and more nurses are deciding to leave the bedside and start their own nurse entrepreneurship journeys. Nurse entrepreneurship is not for everyone, nor is it for the faint of heart. It requires a lot of self-motivation, time management, professionalism, attention to detail, critical thinking, communication skills, and the desire to do the right thing for patients just to name a few. Although you do not necessarily need a business background such as nurse administration, it is certainly helpful. To nurses that are considering the nurse entrepreneurship route, I would say know your WHY. Your why will be what allows you to push through late nights and early mornings. Your WHY will make you get out of bed and make 15 phone calls, receive 15 NO's, and do it again the next day. Your WHY will help you focus on sharing your knowledge, expertise, and gifts to the world, even when the world doesn't yet know they need what you have to offer.

Invest in a business coach that is where you want to be, to help you learn and provide mentorship. Business coaches strive to guide you so that you do not make mistakes that they, or many new entrepreneurs make. Be coachable, and stay up to date in your area of business. There are some outstanding business coaches out there. Take your time, do your homework on the ones that resonate with you. You may find that you will have several coaches. I have three, and they all direct, push, and hold me accountable based on their area of expertise, such as marketing, coaching, or consulting. Some business coaches are nurses that only work with nurses, with the sole mission of helping nurses succeed in the business world by packaging your expertise and knowledge to provide solutions to healthcare organizations.

I would also tell you that if your sole purpose is to get rich overnight, if ever, the entrepreneurship route may not be for you. Nurse entrepreneurship is not a get-rich-quick scheme by any stretch of the imagination. However, it is the result of years of hard work, sweat, tears, tenacity, and a love for what you decide to pursue in business. You do however need to make a living, so keeping your expectations and money goals in perspective by reviewing and updating as needed is essential. Ensure that you have the proper business entity and licenses needed for your particular business. Challenge yourself daily, meet SMART goals, and celebrate your wins, even the small ones. Remember that God wouldn't give you the vision if he didn't think that you were the person to carry that vision out.

About The Author

April McGraw is a nephrology nurse with 18 years of experience. Her educational background includes a BSN from Chamberlain College of Nursing. April has a love and passion for empowering patients to live life to their fullest ability, despite their chronic illness. Combining her nursing experience and personal dialysis experience, she founded iKARE Renal Solutions; a renal consulting agency that helps healthcare organizations provide an increased level of education and support to improve quality incomes, as well as patient experience. Adding a strong desire to provide solutions to patient problems in the renal space, she has added value to each organization and client that she has worked with. As a resident of Hampton Roads Virginia, April is happily married. She and her husband Johnny have two adult children and three grandchildren.

To Contact April McGraw:

Email: info@ikarerenal.com

IG/FB/LinkedIN: ikarerenalsolutions

Always on Duty

By: Lakesha Reed-Curtis MSN, RN

So, you are a Nurse and now you want more? I totally get it. I was once in your shoes, wanting more and just trying to figure out a way to live out my dreams. Nine years later I am doing just that. Let me give you a little information about myself, before I dive in. I am Lakesha Curtis MSN, RN and the President/owner of Allied Health Academy, Medical Solutions Academy, Inc. which was founded in 2011, real-estate investor, dream chasing bad chick. I have an amazing thirteen-year old son, Keshaun, and a beautiful baby girl, Madison, and have been married to my adoring husband Terrel for six years. I have been a Registered Nurse for eighteen years and received both my Bachelor and Master degrees in Nursing at Winston-Salem State University. Currently, I am working on my DNP from American Sentinel University.

Now if you want to know why I chose to be a Nurse, let me tell you. I can't remember my exact age but I was around eleven or twelve. My cousin Courtney and I were at my grandmother's house and he had a nose bleed, so I ran to his aid. I remember my grandmother saying, "Girl, you should be a Nurse." That's right, you know how grandmothers are; any little thing you do right she cheers you on. So she spoke that over my life for the rest of my teenage years and when it was time for me to go to college, my major was nursing. It's funny how things happen in your life and how you can speak things into existence. I don't remember my cousin ever having another nosebleed. Call me crazy, but maybe God allowed that to happen at that particular time so that my grandmother could speak over me. Honestly, if I didn't have that programmed in my head, I don't know where I would be or what I would be doing. Thanks grandma!!!

When it was time for college, I left home for Old Dominion University and managed to stay for one whole semester. Yep...only one semester. I was extremely homesick. I came home for Christmas and never went back, except to retrieve my things. So here I was back at home with my family looking at me crazy, wondering what I was going to do. I applied at my local community college and was accepted into the Practical Nursing Program. I couldn't afford to go straight into RN school because of the time frame. I needed to be finished quickly. Once accepted, my grandma was very ecstatic. I remember telling her one day I may open a school. It was a joke but look at me know. That is an example of putting your dreams out into the universe. I believe that with all my heart. Before you go any further, speak it out in the atmosphere your heart's desires and watch God work. Keep Him close. That's the first step.

Upon completing the Practical Nursing Program, I practiced as a LPN for three years and moved to Hampton, Virginia to purse my RN degree. I received my Associates degree from a local community college and stayed in Hampton for three years before returning back to Danville, Virginia again. I then received my Bachelors from Winston Salem State University. After receiving my Bachelor in Nursing, I eventually moved to Charlotte, North Carolina in hopes of creating more opportunities for me and my son. With this move came a new job opportunity as Assistant Director of Nursing for a company in the Concord area. I was making a pretty decent salary with this company, but I just constantly felt like something was missing. I needed the freedom to live on the edge a little, take business risks, and make my own choices without the constraints of a set schedule or someone else's rules. I don't think people realize how working for someone else consumes your whole life; all other areas are dictated by work because of that tight schedule that comes with it. I was sick of asking for paid time off to take vacations, have a "me" day, or even run errands! And let's be honest, thirty minutes is just not enough time to enjoy a nice lunch. I knew I couldn't work a regular 9-5 job long-term and I needed to make a change quick!

Starting my own business had always been something I wanted to do, but I was skeptical of my own abilities and the great unknown of self-employment. It was time for me to stop feeling like I was missing the mark and do something about the unsettling feeling that had been haunting me daily. I just had to figure out what my niche was. I knew I wanted to help my community in a different way than what was already being done. My main objective was to be constantly learning in whatever I chose to do with the goal of success as the common denominator. Most importantly, I wanted to be home with KeShaun as much as possible once he started school.

I remember working as an Assistant Director of Nursing, making ends meet, but all the while realizing this was not enough sustainable income to take care of me and my son. I mean life was good, don't get me wrong; but I knew it could be better. I needed it to be better. Back then I worked a 9-5 and deeply craved the ability to spend more time with KeShaun. By the time I picked him up from daycare, it would be dark outside and the day was already over. It was during those times I set a goal to be at home with him daily before he started Kindergarten; at the time, he was only two. I would sit around and just pray for a business idea to come to me.

One night as I was lying in bed with my son and the idea of selling scrubs came to me. In that moment, I hugged him so tight and began to jump up and down in the bed! I remember it all so well. I thought big, but started small. I knew my dreams would not allow me to remain small and growth was in my future. I begin doing trade shows at local nursing homes and sold scrubs to most of my co-workers and nursing friends. Little did I know this was the start of my entrepreneurial journey! My best friend's mother, Sandra Estes, allowed me to have my first trade show at her facility. My good girlfriend would travel with me in my Camry, all squished up and surrounded by the scrubs I was carrying up the road to sell. We still laugh about it to this day! Guess what....I still have that Camry too!

I always liked education and knew I would one day go into nursing education; however, I never imagined I would own my very own school. Selling scrubs was something I did on the side while I worked my full-time job, but the moment that sparked the idea for what would be my life altering business venture was being terminated from my job. As a graduate of nursing school, I quickly recognized that nurse aide programs were becoming a trend in North Carolina. This piqued my interest since I had always had the desire to teach. I quickly began researching the requirements and qualifications necessary to become a nursing instructor. This turned into me submitting my application not only to teach but also to open my own school! Ironically, I was terminated from my job as Assistant Director of Nursing in November 2010 and Medical Solutions Academy opened in April 2011. God is amazing! To this day I wonder if I would not have gotten fired, would I have been brave enough to quit the job and follow my dream? It's hard for me to say, but at the time my back was against the wall. I refused to let another individual or company determine the fate of me and my family. In my eyes, I had no other options so I stepped out on faith and started MSA.

Although being an entrepreneur has granted me the desired freedom to work as I please, we all know being the boss is not easy! Couple that with being a mom and a wife and you have reached a completely new level of being on demand for your time. Every woman will have her own set of rules and guidelines she lives by to balance her everyday life. My one and only rule is God, family, and THEN business. I live by this and try my best to follow this day in and day out. Anytime I tend to stray from this line of order, it seems like my whole world turns upside down. When things tend to go wrong, I check myself to make sure I'm following my golden rule. If I find that I've switched that order, I'll immediately start praying and ask God to align my vision to his again. My purpose in starting my business was given to me through the talents with which God blessed me and He will forever come first in my life. My family is and will always be my main priority on Earth; therefore, although my business is my baby, it will always come third in my life.

When I was terminated from my job, I was already in the process of submitting my paperwork to the Board of Nursing to have my Nurse Aide program approved. During this time my life was very stressful. I was in the process of buying a house, I had just lost my job and my lease was running out on my apartment. The broker of my home was telling me to find another job so that I wouldn't lose my house, but I refused. I had faith and was determined God would see me through; however, I did find a part-time job teaching at a local Nurse Aide school. I only worked there for about 2 months because my program was approved. Not to mention I was moving into my new home.

In order to move forward with this program, I had to have a building. A local realtor allowed me to use the address on my paperwork until I was approved without paying anything. So, as soon as my program was approved with a pending site visit, I literally had to set my school up within a week. I had been purchasing equipment along the way, so it wasn't too bad. Now my first building/school was very small. It consisted of three rooms, which were not connected. I painted those rooms my favorite royal blue color and was on my way. I was so proud. I was also thankful to God most of all for seeing this through. My major goal was to be at home with my son daily once he started Kindergarten, but I was able to be home once he started Pre-K which was even sooner than planned. God is amazing!

Once my school opened in Danville, Virginia, I was blessed with a full class from the start. I really believe this was because I put a little buzz in the community a couple of months before I opened. You will have some people who say don't tell others your dreams. I am the opposite; if you know your dreams are going to happen, then tell someone. You just don't want to open a business and no one has any idea that you were about to open. Word of mouth is always a good marketing tool especially in a tight knit community.

When I initially opened, I had a secretary and worked 16 hours a day for the first year. I taught the day and evening classes. I was so tired, but it was the most fulfilling thing I had ever done. For once, I really was the BOSS. Now I don't want you to think that being a nursepreneur is all glitz and glamour. It is hard work, but dreams do become a reality if you put in the effort. This was actually the hardest, but yet most fulfilling thing I had ever done. I don't want you to get confused and think those times will not come and you have no one to talk to and you are in the closet crying. The ugly cry. You will broke at times because business is slow or you have just invested a lot of money in your business. Let me tell you this, money should be the least of your worries. You have the money in your brain and you will reap the benefits of your labor sooner than you think. Just get started. Slow progress is better than no progress. You don't want to have the what-ifs lingering in your head.

After the first year, I was finally able to hire staff and return to my home in North Carolina. Yep, I opened a business two hours away from my home in Charlotte back in my hometown. Now this part of my entrepreneur journey is the hardest. If my staff gets low; I may have to stay away from home a couple of days. If things go array, I cannot be there in a blink of an eye because I live far away. I did however stay in Virginia for the last two years to develop my Practical Nursing program. I sometimes think about moving back closer to my establishment, but that would defeat the purpose of being an entrepreneur. I like the freedom and I should be able to work from anywhere in the world. Only God knows the where I will end up living permanently.

Medical Solutions Academy now has a Practical Nursing, Nurse Aide, Medication Aide, Medical Office Assistant, Medical Assistant, CPR, and Patient Care Technician. I am also in the process of becoming accredited.

Giving up honestly has never been a thought to cross my mind. I do have those moments when I say forget this, I am going to find a job; however, I get over that in 20-30 minutes flat. Who would I be kidding? I am an entrepreneur by nature and at heart. The process does get hard and you will face a lot of adversity. Sometimes it comes from those closest to you. But if God can see you to it, He will see you through it. I have moments when I question myself. Who am I to start a school and have all of these big dreams and goals? But as I knock those goals out, I am quickly reminded of who I am... Lakesha Reed- Curtis, a dreamer and a doer. I honestly believe there is nothing I cannot accomplish with God, the right team, and the right mindset. This is something you must remember - nothing great can be done alone and you have to pay to play. Don't try to get everything done for free. Words that my husband always tells me are, "You get what you pay for." This is so true. Invest, Invest, Invest in your business! I cannot stress this enough. It is also important to have a good lawyer and accountant in your corner early on. I wish someone would have told me that before getting started in business, but this is one of the many lessons I have learned along the way.

I also suggest having multiple streams of income. Medical Solutions Academy is my bread and butter. However, I like to invest in real estate. Renovating properties has become a passion of mine. It is now a second business. It is a lot of work, but I love to seem something that was once deemed unsuitable to live in, a warm and cozy place for someone to call their home.

You will face many obstacles on your path to entrepreneurship, but passion will take you where you need to go. When you stay focused and put your all into your dreams, it begins to feel as if your back is against the wall. You will either fold and go back to working for someone else, or you will be driven that much more to continue on your pursuit of reaching your goals. No matter how difficult my journey had gotten, turning back was never an option for me. I had my son depending on me and I was determined to not only be a good mom, but to also be present as much as possible. I already had the passion for Nursing. Coupled with the desire to be at home with my son as much as possible, these two factors gave me the motivation I needed to see my dreams come to fruition.

If you can control the way your mind thinks of being a Nursepreneur, I strongly believe you will make it through the process. Too often we allow self-doubt and fear creep into our minds and gain control of our thoughts. All of a sudden, what once seemed easy now seems impossible all because of negative thinking. We are our own biggest enemy in life. Next thing you know, you're convincing yourself not to quit your job and go into business for yourself because it seems illogical. If you focus on what could go wrong instead of all the things that are going right, then everything will fall apart quicker than you could ever imagine. You have to have faith in yourself and on the days you can't put faith in yourself, put it in God because there is absolutely nothing he cannot do. What is meant for you is for you and no one can deter you from receiving your blessings. I am always looking for new ways to build my empire and leave a legacy for my family. As you can see, I AM ALWAYS ON DUTY.

About The Author

Mrs. Lakesha Reed- Curtis, wife and mother of two, is a woman of action who Dreams Big and just decided to Chase Hers! She was born and raised in Danville, Virginia, but now currently resides in Charlotte, North Carolina with her loving family. Her focus in life has always been to find different avenues with the opportunity to provide services to the community. Her goal then became to provide higher education opportunities for students interested in the healthcare field to advance career wise in the future. By introducing Medical Solutions Academy to her community, she has become dedicated to empowering her community through educational programs that serve to make prospective health care workers prepared for employment in the medical field.

Lakesha Curtis has eighteen years of hands-on nursing experience and received both her Bachelor and Master degree from Winston-Salem State University She is currently enrolled at American Sentinel University obtaining her DNP in Nurse Educational Leadership. By establishing Medical Solutions Academy, she has gained adequate experience in the full process of operating and administrating successful medical certification programs from start to finish. She has had the opportunity to witness students complete these certification programs over the course of the last nine years. Her educational program has expanded over the years and now includes Nurse Aide, Medical Assistant, Medication Aide, Medical Office Assistant, CPR Certification, LPN, and soon the LPN to RN bridge program. She has built this school from the ground up and enjoys playing such an important role in others' lives.

To Contact Lakesha Reed-Curtis:

Email: info@dreamchashers.com

LinkedIN- Lakesha Reed-Curtis MSN, RN

Made in the USA
Middletown, DE
19 July 2022